平 面 国

〔英〕艾勃特⊙著

杜景平⊙译

台海出版社

图书在版编目(CIP)数据

平面国 /（英）艾勃特著；杜景平译 . — 北京：
台海出版社，2018.9

ISBN 978-7-5168-2059-9

Ⅰ.①平…　Ⅱ.①艾… ②杜… Ⅲ.①科学幻想小说
—英国—现代 Ⅳ.① I561.45

中国版本图书馆 CIP 数据核字（2018）第 189532 号

平面国

著　者：〔英〕艾勃特		译　者：杜景平
责任编辑：武　波　童媛媛		装帧设计：同人内文化传媒 · 书装设计
版式设计：同人内文化传媒 · 书装设计		责任印制：蔡　旭

出版发行：台海出版社

地　　址：北京市东城区景山东街 20 号　　邮政编码：100009

电　　话：010 -- 64041652（发行，邮购）

传　　真：010 — 84045799（总编室）

网　　址：www.taimeng.org.cn/thcbs/default.htm

E-mail：thcbs@126.com

经　　销：全国各地新华书店

印　　刷：三河市宏顺兴印刷有限公司

本书如有破损、缺页、装订错误，请与本社联系调换

开　　本：710mm×1000mm　　　　1/16

字　　数：152 千字　　　　　　　　印　　张：12.75

版　　次：2018年11月第1版　　　　印　　次：2018年11月第1次印刷

书　　号：ISBN 978-7-5168-2059-9

定　　价：28.80 元

致

空间国所有居民

尤其是上流阶层

本书

由平面国一位卑微公民所著

尽管他自己曾领略过

三维之国的魅力

但由于一直以来习惯

二维世界

他希望

那神奇国度的人们

将不断探索新知

并掌握四维、五维、六维

直至七维世界的奥秘

从而

开启我们的想象空间

同时

在立体世界的

上层社会中

培养出那罕见的美德——

谦逊

译者序

埃德温·A.艾勃特（1838—1926）是英国的一位神学家、作家，曾担任历史悠久的伦敦城市中学校长。他毕业于剑桥大学圣约翰学院。

从剑桥大学毕业后，他先后在爱德华国王学校和克利夫顿学院任教。1865年，他被任命为伦敦城市中学校长（该校也是他的母校），任职长达24年，直到1889年退休。他退休时年龄只有50岁。退休后，他没有放弃工作，而是开始全身心投入写作。

埃德温·A.艾勃特的写作题材涉猎广泛。他的主要作品包括《平面国》（1884年）、《莎士比亚文法》（1870年）、《英国语文》（1871年）和《如何提高写作》（1872年）。他还是研究弗朗西斯·培根的著名专家，曾出版《培根和埃塞克斯》（1877年），并为《培根随笔》（1886年）撰写了导读。

《平面国》（英文全名为Flatland: A Romance of Many Dimensions），是埃德温·A.艾勃特的代表作，出版于1884年。它是一部具有讽刺意味的科幻小说，同时也是一本关于空间几何知识的科普读物。

小说主人公自称是一个正方形，出生于平面国，里面居住着各种平面图形。书的第一部分，正方形通过自己的视角介绍了平面国的气候、建筑、人口、法律、政治等社会风貌。这些生动有趣的描述，无情地揭露和讽刺了英国维多利亚时代的社会等级制度。作者用各种平面图形类比现实生活中社会各阶层的人物，令读者拍案叫绝，而对社会制度鞭辟入里的评析又令人哑然失笑。书的第二部分讲述了正方形如何获得三维知识，然后又如何试图向平面国其他人传播该福音的奇幻故事。该部分对人类（尤其是上层社会）的高傲无知进行了辛辣的嘲讽。正如作者在前言中所说，本书的目的就是要在"上层社会中培养出那罕见的美德——谦逊"。

《平面国》已经被改编成了《平面国》（2007）、《平面国2：球体国》（2012）等多部电影。

杜景平

2018年4月

目　录

第一部分　我的世界

第二部分　其他世界

第一部分　我的世界

"不要懊恼，这是一个广大的世界。"[1]

[1] 出自英国伟大剧作家威廉·莎士比亚著名戏剧《罗密欧与朱丽叶》（第三幕，第三场）。——译者注

I 平面国的本质

我将我们的世界称为平面国，并非因为这是它的名称，而是为了让您——有幸居住在空间里的快乐读者们——更容易看清它的本质。

假设一张巨大的纸上铺着直线、三角形、正方形、五边形、六边形以及其他图形。它们并非静止不动，而是在纸面上自由行走，但不能脱离纸面，就像影子一样——只不过是带着清晰的亮边。这样你就能正确理解我的国家和人民了。啊，要是在几年以前，我会说"我的宇宙"，但是现在我对事物有更深刻的认识了。

你会立刻发现，在这样的一个国度里不存在任何能称为"立体的"物体，但是我敢说，你会认为我们至少可以凭借视觉来区分移动中的三角形和正方形，以及其他图形。恰恰相反，我们无法看到这种情形，更别提区分它们了。除了直线之外，我们什么都看不见。我还是赶紧解释下这是为什么吧。

请在你们空间国的桌子中央放置一枚便士，然后你从它的正上方往下看，它会呈现出一个圆形。

现在请把你的头移到桌子的边沿，然后徐徐地降低自己的视线（这样你就逐渐进入平面国居民的状态了），你会发现便士的形状在慢慢变成椭圆，最后当你的视线和桌面完全平齐时（此时，你就完全成了平面国的居民），你看见的便士就不再是椭圆形，而是一条直线了。

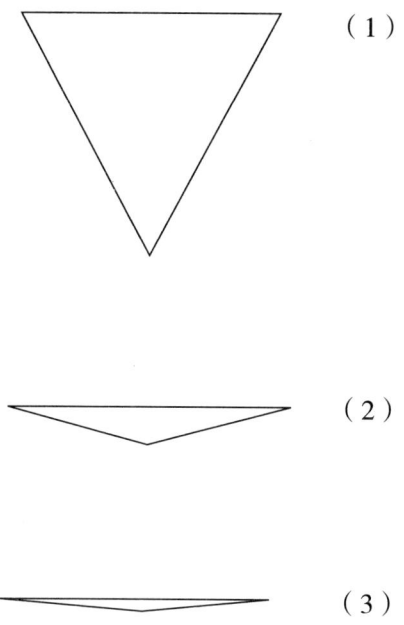

（1）

（2）

（3）

　　要是你用同样的方法观察用纸板剪成的三角形，正方形，或者任何其他图形，结果都会相同。只要你的视线和桌面保持平齐，所有的图形都不再是它们的原状，而是变成直线。让我们以等边三角形（在我们平面国里，他们代表受人尊敬的商人阶层）为例。图（1）是你从正上方看到的商人的模样，图（2）是你的视线接近桌面时看到的，图（3）则是视线几乎和桌面平齐时的所见。要是你的视线和桌面完全平齐（也就是我们在平面国里看他们的角度），你能看见的就只有一条直线。

　　我在空间国里听说你们的水手在海上远航时也会有类似的体验，他们很难分辨远处地平线上的岛屿和海岸。远处的大陆上也许有大小不一，形状各异的海湾、陆岬以及海角，但是从远处你根本无法看清它们，除非充足的阳光正好将它们照射得轮廓清晰、阴阳分明，否则你能看见的只是水平线上那一条连绵不断的灰色线条。

　　嘿嘿，这就是平面国里的三角形或者其他熟人朝我们走来时我们看到的情形。由于我们这儿既没有太阳，也没有光线投射阴影，所以我们没法看见空间国里呈现的立体视图。当我们的朋友走近我们时，他的直线就会变大；反之，它就变小。但是无论他是三角形、正方形、五边形、六边形，还是圆形，他的形状始终都是一条直线。

您也许会问在如此困难的环境下，我们是如何能将朋友们区分开来的。其实，当我开始描绘平面国的居民生活状况时，你会发现这个问题的答案很简单。现在，让我暂时换一个话题，先和你聊一聊我们国家的气候和房屋吧。

II 平面国的气候和房屋

正如你们的指南针一样，我们的也有四个方向：东西南北。

由于没有太阳和任何其他天体，我们无法用常规的方法辨别方向。但是我们有自己的一套办法。由于我们平面国的自然引力，所有物体都会始终具有向南运动的趋势。尽管在气候温和的地区，这种引力很微弱（健康状况良好的妇女能够不用太费力就可以向北走动几弗朗[1]），但是在我们平面国，这种向南引力足够使指南针发挥作用。另外，由于雨水永远都是每隔一定时间从北边降落，所以这也能帮助我们辨别方向。在城里，我们可以借助房屋辨认方向，因为房屋的边墙多半是东西朝向，所以屋顶可以遮挡从北边降落的雨水。在乡下，由于没有房屋，树干可以充当我们的向导。因而，在测定方位时，我们并没有你们想象中的那么麻烦。

然而，在气候不甚理想的地方，我们几乎感受不到向南的引力。有时走在荒无人烟的开阔地区，由于没有任何房屋和树木给我做向导，我不得不停下脚步，原地不动待上几个小时，直到开始下雨，我才能继续我的行程。然而对于老弱者而言，尤其是纤弱的女性，向南的引力要比对强壮的男性的影响大得多。因此，在街上遇到女士，让她走在你的北侧是一种个人修养。然而当你身体健康，又处在一个很难辨清方向的环境时，能做到这一点绝非易事。

我们的房屋没有任何窗户，因为无论室内室外，白天黑夜都有

---

[1] 弗朗是英国使用的长度单位，1弗朗相当于201米。——译者注

光线，它们无时无刻，无处不在。至于其原因，我们不得而知。古时候，光的起源问题对博学的人而言是个有趣而值得经常探究的话题。时不时也有人尝试给出答案，但是结果是这些异想天开的人把我们的疯人院挤满了。最初，立法机构试图通过高额征税打击那些钻研这个问题的人，但是效果不甚理想，因此，最近他们索性完全禁止人们对此再进行讨论。啊，虽然我是平面国里唯一知道这个神秘问题答案的人，但是我无法让我任何一个同胞理解它，于是他们冷嘲热讽我这个唯一掌握了空间真理，并且从三维世界里盗取知识火种的人。仿佛我是最癫狂的人！唉，还是不说这些令人伤心的话吧，让我们再回到房屋这个话题。

　　房屋最常见的形状是五边形，正如下图所示。北侧的两条边RO和OF构成屋顶，屋顶多半没有门。东墙上有一扇专为女性开的小门；西墙有一扇专为男性开的大门；南边也称为地板，通常没有门。

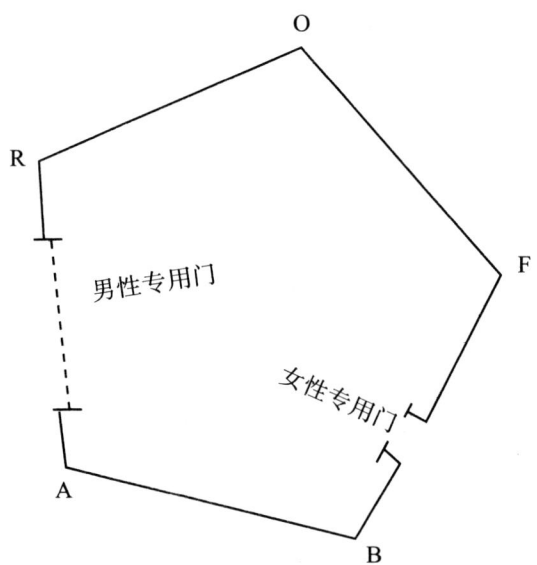

　　正方形和三角形的房屋是被禁止的，其原因如下：正方形的角（以及等边三角形的角）比五边形的要尖锐得多，而无生命物体（例

如房屋）的边线又比人类的轮廓更模糊。所以平面国规定房屋不能建成正方形或者三角形，以免粗心或者开小差的路人撞上屋角而受伤。早在十一世纪，法律就明文禁止建造三角形的房屋，只有以下建筑例外：防御工事、火药库、部队营房以及其他公共建筑。这些建筑都是普通大众不得轻易靠近的。

在那一段时间里，正方形房屋可以随意建造，只不过需要缴纳特种税。但是，大约过了三百年，出于公共安全考虑，法律又规定在所有人口超过一万的城市里，房屋的屋角不得小于标准五边形的角。民众也很通情达理，并支持了立法机构的决定。现在即使在乡下，五边形房屋也已经替代了其他房屋形状。只有在偏远落后的乡野，也许考古爱好者还能发现方形的房屋。

III 关于平面国的居民

平面国居民的最高身高大约为十一英寸[1]。十二英寸的身高绝对是极限。

我们的妇女们都是直线。

士兵和最底层的工人都是等腰三角形，两边大约为十一英寸长，底边很窄（通常不超过半英寸），所以他们的顶角尖锐而锋利。当他们的底边变得最短时（不超过1/8英寸），他们的顶角会就变得极其尖锐，导致我们很难将他们和直线或者妇女区分开。和你们使用的称呼一样，我们也将他们称为等腰三角形。在下文中，我就用这个名字称呼他们。

中等阶级由等边三角形或者正三角形组成。

我们的专业人士和绅士阶层包括正方形（我本人就属于正方形）和五边形。

再往上就是贵族，他们分为多个级别。第一级别是六边形，贵族们每增加一条边，就上升一个级别，最高级别为多边形。当一个图形的边数越大，边长就越短，最终就变得像一个圆，然后他就进入了圆形或者牧师的等级，即社会最高阶层。

平面国的自然定律是每一个男孩都会比他父亲多一条边，因此每一代人都比他们的上一代向贵族阶层靠近了一步。这就意味着正方形的儿子是五边形，五边形的儿子是六边形，以此类推。

---

[1] 1英寸（in）= 2.54厘米（cm）。

但是这个定律对商人不是总能适用，更不用说对士兵和工人，因为他们的三条边不一样长，所以几乎不能算作人。于是，自然定律在他们身上也不起作用，等腰三角形的儿子依然是等腰三角形。然而，他们也并非毫无希望，等腰三角形的后代也有步入上流社会的微小机会。因为，经过长期军营生活的历练，或者常年辛勤的劳作，工匠和士兵阶层中最聪明的那些人的底边会逐渐变长，而另两条边会缩短。这些人的子女通婚（由牧师安排）后生育的后代会变得更像等边三角形阶层。

等腰三角形的后代人口众多，且几乎依然都是等腰三角形，他们的后代中出现被认证[1]为等边三角形的情况非常罕见。要生育出等边三角形后代，不但需要通过一系列精心安排的通婚，他们的先辈还要长年累月地勤俭节约、克己自律，而且只有经过等腰三角形家庭几代人耐心、系统而持续的智力提升后才有可能实现。

如果有等腰三角形父母产下一个经过认证的等边三角形婴儿，这条新闻就会成为附近乡里的美谈。经过卫生部门和社会委员会的严格检查后，如果婴儿确认是等边三角形，他们会为他举行一个晋升等边三角形阶层的庄重仪式。之后他们会立刻从那既自豪又伤心的亲生父母身边将这个孩子抱走，送给无子的等边三角形家庭领养，后者还要发誓绝不再让这个孩子踏入他的亲生父母家半步，以免这个涉世未深的懵懂小孩因为下意识地模仿亲戚的行为举止而再次沦落到原来的底层社会。

农奴出生的父母偶尔生育出等腰三角形子女是这些贫困的农奴们

---

[1] 空间国的评论家可能会问："为什么需要认证？难道生育一个正方形儿子不就能证明父亲就是等边三角形吗？"对此，我的回答是：任何阶层的女性都不会嫁给一个没有经过身份认证的三角形。正方形的后代有时是由完全规则的三角形生育的，但是这种情况下，第一代为三角形的不规则情形几乎都在第三代中出现，这样一来他们的第三代可能不能晋升为五边形阶层，甚至可能退回到三角形阶层。

盼望的喜事，因为这会给他们低贱卑微的生活带来一线希望和光明，而且也会受到大多数贵族阶层的欢迎，因为这种罕见的现象不但几乎不会对他们的特权产生任何影响，反而正是防止底层民众发动革命的最有利障碍。

倘若所有长着锐角的底层阶级都被剥夺改变命运的希望和梦想，他们反而会从革命活动中寻找到自己的领袖人物，然后在这些领袖人物的领导下，人口众多的底层阶级就可能打败智力占优的圆形阶层。但是有一条自然法则规定，工人阶层每增长一点智慧、知识以及品德，他们的内角度数就会相应增加，直到接近无害的等边三角形的度数（如此一来，他们的身形就变得异常笨拙）。因此，在争勇好斗的下等士兵阶层（他们的智力却和妇女一样低下）中，我们能够发现他们每增长一分攻城拔寨的勇猛，同时就会失去一分运筹帷幄的智慧。

自然界的补偿定律是多么的不可思议啊！平面国里贵族阶层天生高贵，这又是对适者生存法则多么完美的诠释啊！通过充分抓住人们向往美好生活的心理弱点，多边形和圆形阶层就可以熟练操控这条自然法则，将各种革命扼杀在摇篮中。除了自然法则有利之外，他们还有很多科技手段。只要御医们稍微施展人体压缩和拉伸技术，他们就可以让一些识时务的革命首领变得温驯无比，然后将他们诏安进特权阶级。于是，革命首领手下那些不甚聪明的头目们，在这种待遇的诱惑下，被诱骗至公立医院后遭到终身软禁。倘若其中有一两个无可救药的顽固分子，还会被他们直接灭口。

再后来，这些等腰三角形阶层的乌合之众，要么就会陷于群龙无首状态，最终被圆形首领豢养的职业政客们打击得毫无还击之力，要么就被圆形政党挑拨离间后，陷入互相残杀的境地，最终死于自己人的角下。在我们的史书上记载的革命次数不少于一百二十次，而小规模的骚乱则多达两百三十五起，但是它们均没有逃过这种宿命。

IV 关于妇女

如果顶角锋利的三角形士兵已算得上是令人生畏，那么我们的妇女们则比他们还要可怕得多。如果士兵是楔子，妇女则是长针，因为她们的两头完全是锋芒毕露。这种特性使得她们几乎可以随心所欲地隐形，因此，在平面国里，你会发现妇女是根本惹不起的动物。

也许年轻的读者会问，平面国的妇女如何能将自己隐形。我觉得，其中原因显而易见，无须解释。然而，我还是要啰唆两句，让那些头脑简单的人一听就明白。

请在桌上放一根针，然后将你的视线和桌面平齐，从针的两侧看过去，你会看到它的整个长度，但是如果你顺着针头看过去，你就只能看见一个点，所以说这枚针近乎隐形了。我们的妇女就是如此。当她以侧身示人时，我们看到的是一条直线，当她以长着眼睛和嘴巴（这两个器官长得完全一样）的头部示人时，那么我们能看见的就是一个亮点；倘若是她们的脚先映入我们的眼帘，我们看到的一个不太明亮的小点，她们的脚像无生命的物体一样模糊不清，如同一个隐形的帽子一般。

空间国里智商最平庸的人也能立刻意识到妇女会给我们造成巨大的危害。在平面国里，中等阶级中受人尊敬的等边三角形的锐角十分危险；撞上工人会擦伤皮肤；撞到军官更会严重受伤；触摸列兵的顶角则有生命危险，而撞上一位妇女，则必定当场殒命！倘若妇女是隐形的，或者只是一个不太起眼的模模糊糊的小点，即使是最谨慎的人，也难以做到绝不与之相撞！

因此，平面国的很多州在不同时期都颁布了法令，尽量降低这种意外发生的概率。在南方以及气候不甚温和的地区，由于引力要比别处更强烈，人们也更容易随意移动，因而针对妇女的法律也要严格得多。从以下几条法律条款中我们就能对整个法律的苛刻略知一二。

1. 每一栋房屋必须在东边设一入口，只允许女性进出；她们必须"以合适而得体的方式进入"[1]，且绝对不允许从专为男性而设的西门进出。

2. 任何女性进入公共场所时必须不停地发出善意的叫声，否则将面临死刑。

3. 任何女性，一旦确诊患有圣维特斯舞蹈症、痉挛、长期伴有剧烈喷嚏的感冒，或者任何导致无法自控行为的疾病，都将被立即处死。

有一些州，还另有法律规定女性进入或者待在公共场所时必须不停左右摇晃她们的后背，以提醒背后的人，否则她们将面临死刑；有些州则强迫女性外出时，身后必须跟着自己的一个儿子、仆人或者是丈夫；还有些州索性禁止女性外出，只有宗教节日时除外。但是我们最聪明的圆形阶层以及政治家们已经发现，严加控制女性行为不但导致了女性人口的减少，而且也助长了家庭谋杀案的上升，以致这种严苛的法律其实得不偿失。

因为，每当妇女们无法再忍受被禁锢在家中或者外出时面临的各种限制，她们的愤怒就会猛然爆发，于是她们就将自己的怨恨一股脑儿发泄在自己的丈夫和孩子身上。在气候不太温和的地区，曾经发生过全村的男性在一两个小时内被同时暴怒的妇女集体消灭的惨案。因

---

[1] 我在空间国的时候，发现你们有一些牧师会为村民、替人摇扇子的人以及寄宿学校的老师们（1884年9月出版的《旁观者》杂志，第1255页有此记载）专门设置一道门，好让他们"以合适而得体的方式进入"。

此，以上提及的三个法律条例，在管理良好的州已经足够，也可以被视作涉及妇女法律的典范。

总之，我们的安全保障不是由立法机构提供的，而是由妇女们自己的利益决定的。因为，尽管她们可以随时用极端的行为让别人瞬间丧命，但是同时她们也必须考虑用尖头刺伤他人时，是否能腾出手脚来自卫，因为此时她们也很容易受到攻击。

社会风尚对我们也颇为有利。前文中，我已说过在一些文明程度不高的州郡，妇女必须在公众场合中不停地左右摇摆自己的后背。自从平面国的人有记忆以来，在治理有序的州郡里，扭动腰肢的做法在那些自视教养甚好的妇女们当中相当普遍。对于上层妇女而言，这种行为规范已成为了一种本能。因此，一旦有任何妇女受到以上法律条款惩罚，都会被视作整个州的奇耻大辱。圆形阶层妇女富有节奏地扭动腰肢的动作受到普通等边三角形阶层妻子们狂热的推崇和模仿。其实后者除了学到了像钟摆一样的动作之外，并无其他收获。于是，等边三角形妇女的摇曳身姿又不折不扣地被等腰三角形中那些有上进心和理想的妇女们效仿。然而，这些妇女其实根本没有任何机会进入公共场合，因而也就没有机会展示她们曼妙的身姿。如此一来，摇曳腰肢已然成为一种社会风尚；而这些妇女的丈夫和孩子们也乐观其成，因为，这样他们可以免受她们突如其来的攻击。

以上情况的出现并非因为女性生性如此冷酷无情，而是因为这些脆弱而不幸的女性所有的行为都由激情控制。由于她们不配长有任何外角，地位甚至低于社会最底层的等腰三角形，因此，她们完全缺乏智商，既没有思考能力和判断力，也不会未雨绸缪，甚至记忆力也几乎为零。正因如此，当她们愤怒的时候，就会完全失去理智，变得丧心病狂。我曾听闻一起惨案：一个妇女盛怒之下将全家人杀害，清醒之后还将家人尸体清扫得干干净净。可是不过半个小时，她居然问别人自己丈夫和孩子是死于何人之手！

　　显然，在女性们能够自由转身的场合，千万不要惹恼她们。然而在她们自己家里，你倒是可以畅所欲言，因为她们的房屋结构限制了她们的攻击行为。此时，她们完全没有能力袭击他人，即便有此想法，她们要么很快就会忘记自己攻击别人的原因，要么将你为了哄骗她们而做出的那些允诺早就忘得一干二净。

　　总的说来，除了军队里下层士兵之间的关系不好相处之外，我们平面国的家庭关系颇为和睦。在家里，有些丈夫由于缺乏察言观色的智慧，因而会莫名其妙地招致杀身之祸。而在室外，另一些鲁莽的丈夫们却因为高估了自己锋利的锐角，而不是审时度势或者适时装憨以求明哲保身，以至于要么经常忘记给自己妻子的住房进行特殊的设计，要么经常被他人误导而对妻子说错话，结果总是惹怒她们。此外，由于他们总爱讲一些不切实际的大道理，又不会像圆滑世故的圆形阶层那样用花言巧语讨好他们的配偶，如此一来，结果总是丈夫惨遭屠杀。就这样，那些愚蠢而令人讨厌的等腰三角形丈夫被消灭了，而这一结果也并不是没有益处。其实，很多圆形阶层人士认为妇女的攻击性正是淘汰多余人口，将革命扼杀在摇篮中的一种便捷方法。

　　但是，即使在我们最顶层的圆形阶层家庭里，我也不敢说他们理想的家庭生活能和你们空间国里的相媲美。尽管他们的家中没有杀戮，因而勉强算得上太平，但是夫妻之间却绝少有情投意合和趣味相投。精于算计的圆形阶层以牺牲舒适的家庭生活为代价换取了各自的安全。自古以来，在圆形阶层或者多边形家庭中就养成了一个习惯（现在已然成为我们上流社会女性的一种本能）——母亲和女儿们的眼睛和嘴巴必须时刻盯着她们的丈夫或者男性朋友。要是一位贵妇人用背对着她的丈夫，我们几乎可以肯定她很快将面临被抛弃的命运。但是，下面我会讲到，这种习俗尽管能保障家庭安全，但也并非没有缺陷。

在工人或者令人尊敬的商人家里，当妻子们在家里自娱自乐的时候，她们可以背对她们的丈夫。只有此时，家里才会获得片刻的宁静，因为她们终于在丈夫眼前消失，不再唠唠叨叨，只是不停地发出欢快的哼哼声。但是在上层阶级的家庭里，几乎没有任何安静时刻。妻子喋喋不休的嘴巴和老鹰般的眼睛总是围绕着房屋的主人打转。她们的话没完没了，无休无止。就算你有预防被妻子针头刺死的智慧和手段，也拿她们的嘴巴完全没有任何办法。即使她们说的都是废话，但由于缺乏智商和自觉性，她们根本就不会自动停止唠叨。据说，一些愤世嫉俗的人士曾讲过，他们宁可被妻子看不见的针头刺死，也不愿被她们看似安全的唠叨轰炸而亡。

在空间国的读者看来，平面国女性的生活无比凄惨，而事实也的确如此。最低等的等腰三角形男性至少还可以祈盼自己的内角度数能够有所增加，直到最终有一天能改变子孙后代的命运。但是妇女们却没有任何类似的希望。"一朝为妇，终身为妇"，这便是自然法则。自然进化论仿佛在她们身上不起任何作用。然而，我们至少可以为上天的安排感到欣慰，因为它规定，既然她们的人生没有任何希望，因此也就没有回忆，没有期盼。她们的悲惨和屈辱是自身生存的前提条件，也是整个平面国的立国之本。

V 关于我们如何彼此辨识

你们有幸长着双眼，能看见光线和阴影，还具备透视知识，能欣赏到各种迷人的色彩。你们可以在快乐的三维国度里看见角度，计算圆的周长。我该如何才能向您讲明白我们平面国的居民相互辨识时面临的重重困难呢？

请您先回忆一下我的前文所述。平面国里所有的物体，不论是有生命的，还是无生命的，无论其形状如何，在我们眼中几乎都只有一个模样，即直线的形状。既然所有物体都长得一样，那我们到底是如何区分彼此的呢？

我们一共有三种方法。首先，我们通过听觉辨别。我们的听觉比你们要发达得多，它不但可以让我们通过声音辨识出自己的朋友，甚至可以区分出不同的社会阶层，至少是最底层的三个阶层：等边三角形，正方形和五边形（我没有将等腰三角形计算在内）。社会等级越高，凭听觉识人就越难，一部分原因是声音容易雷同，另一部分原因是虽然平民百姓擅长听音识人，而贵族阶层却不太善于此道。凡是听音识人碰到困难时，我们就不再依赖这种方法。在下层社会中，发声的能力远比听觉发达，所以一个等腰三角形可以轻而易举地模仿多边形的嗓音，甚至稍加训练还可冒充圆形的声音。因此，第二种方法使用更为常见。

现在我要说说我们的妇女和上层阶级。在他们之间，触摸是最主要的认人方式。这种方法不仅在陌生人之间使用，而且也不仅是个别人使用，而是整个阶层都是如此。空间国里上层人士的相互介绍过程就是我们的互相"触摸"的过程。例如，"请允许我邀请您触摸，并被我的朋友某某先生触摸"，这种说法依然在偏远农村的老派乡绅中使用，这也是平面国里介绍朋友的标准句式。但是在城里的商人之间，"被触摸"几个字会被省略，因而整个句子就变成了："请允许我邀请您触摸一下某某先生。"尽管此时，"触摸"显然是相互的。然而，在那些极端痛恨虚情假意的问候，对自己民族语言纯洁性也漠不关心的前卫的年轻绅士们之间，上面的句子又被进一步简化。他们将"触摸"一词变成专有动词，意思是：为了相互触摸而进行介绍。此时，上流社会中的精英人士就会怒斥诸如"史密斯先生，让我介绍[1]您和琼斯先生互相触摸"之类的句子过于粗鲁。

亲爱的读者们，您千万不要以为我们的"触觉"识人方式和你们的方式一样枯燥乏味，也不要以为我们只有在触摸一个人的每一条边之后才能断定他所属的阶层。经过学校和日常生活中的长期练习和训练，我们能够凭借触觉立刻分辨出等腰三角形，正方形和五边形的内角度数。无须多言，即使触觉最迟钝的人也能轻易感觉出智商低下的等腰三角形的顶角。因此，作为一条不成文的规定，我们认人时只需触摸一条边即可断定对方所属的阶级，除非对方是贵族阶层中的上流人士，因为他们很难通过触觉辨别。即便是温特桥大学[2]的文学硕士也曾将十边形和十二边形贵族弄混淆，也没有哪一所大学培养的理学博士能当场毫不费力地分辨出二十边形和二十四边形的贵族。

那些还记得我前文所引述关于妇女法令的读者们，肯定已经发现，通过触摸认识别人的时候必须非常小心谨慎，否则稍有不慎就有

---

[1] 此处原文为permit me to feel you Mr. Jones。——译者注
[2] 温特桥是英国西约克郡首府韦克菲尔德市的一个村庄名称。该村因横穿村庄的温特河（river Went）而得名。温特桥大学系作者杜撰。而温特桥大学系作者杜撰，用来影射剑桥大学（the University of Cambridge），因为剑桥大学即以流经其校园的river Cam（康河）而得名。——译者注

可能遭受不可弥补的伤害。为了确保触摸者的安全，被触摸者应当纹丝不动。此时，身体稍有晃动或者突然打喷嚏，都有可能给触摸者造成致命的后果，而他们之间本来可以建立的友情也将化为乌有。这一点在下层社会的三角形中尤为重要。因为，他们的眼睛远离自己的顶点，所以看不见远端肢体的动作。他们天生反应迟钝，无法感觉到富有教养的多边形的轻微触摸。认识生人时，要是不由自主的摇晃了一下脑袋就导致对方珍贵的生命被剥夺，那将是多么悲哀的事情啊！

　　我听说我那优秀的祖父，曾是不幸福的等腰三角形阶层中最守规矩的一员。虽然在他去世前不久，卫生部门和社会委员会的七票中有四票同意批准他晋升为等边三角形阶层，但是他坚毅的眼眶里总是噙满泪水，因为他的曾曾曾祖父（一位内角为59° 30'的令人尊敬的工人）曾经有机会和他一样获得这份荣誉，但是由于一个小小的失误而错失良机。据我祖父说，我那位不幸的祖先，由于患有风湿病，在一次被一位多边形贵族触摸时，不知何故突然用自己的顶角将对方刺死。后来，也许是因为长期遭监禁而导致自我堕落，也许是由于此事极大地影响了我祖先所有亲属的道德水准，导致我们家族的内角缩减了一度。结果是他子女的内角只有58°，直到经过后面五代人的不懈努力才弥补上了这损失的1°，从而达到60°，家族也最终得以晋升为等边三角形。然而，这所有的灾难竟然是源自那一次触摸时的小小意外！

　　此时，我能听到一些知识渊博的读者在发出质疑的声音："在平面国里，你们如何能知道内角的度数和分数？我们能看见角，那是因为我们身处空间国里，可以看见两条直线相交，但是你们一次只能看见一条直线，或者是看到一条长长的直线上不同的小线段。你们怎么能够区分角，怎么能测量出他们的度数？"

　　我的回答是，虽然我们看不见角，但是可以进行精确地推测。出于生存需要，加之长期的训练，在不借助工具，仅凭视觉的情况下，我们可以比你们更能精确地分辨角度的大小。我也可以坦率告诉你们老天也给予了我们恩赐。自然法则规定，等腰三角形家族的大脑（顶角）从0.5°，即30′开始，然后每繁衍一代人，就增长0.5°，直到长满60°。此时他们的农奴身份才算结束，并以自由人的身份进入等边三角形阶层。

为此，自然给我们提供了从0.5°到60°的刻度表，这个刻度表的三角形标本在平面国的每所小学里都有。由于偶有退化，以及更常见的道德和智力滞涨现象，加上罪犯和流浪汉阶层的人口众多，0.5°和1°的人大量过剩，10°以下的人口人满为患。他们被完全剥夺了人权，其中很多人甚至不具备当兵的智力，因此被各州派去作为样本从事教育服务工作，以免祸害社会。他们被教育委员会安置在小学和幼儿园的教室里，利用他们向中等阶级的子女传授这些可怜虫们自己都完全缺乏的知识和技能。

有些州会偶尔给这些样本提供食物让他们苟延残喘活几年。但是气候温和，治理有序的地区，却不给他们提供食物，而是每月（这个时间间隔也正好是罪犯们在没有食物情况下能生存的平均时长）定期更换一批新的样本，因为长远看来这样更有利于下一代的教育。在学费低廉的学校里，养活这些样本已变得毫无意义，一半原因是他们会消耗粮食，另一半原因是经过数周不断地"触摸"他人而导致他们自身的外角失去了精准度。在列举学费高昂制度的优点时，我们也不应忘记，这种体制在一定程度上有助于消灭多余的等腰三角形人口，而这些人正是平面国里的每一位政客时刻要提防的。尽管我非常清楚很多由选举产生的校董事会都倾向于采取"学费低廉的制度"（这是他们的原话），我觉得这只不过是再次印证了"成本才是经济的最重要因素"这个道理而已。

　　我不想让校董事会的政治问题转移我的话题。我确信，我已经讲得很清楚了，通过触觉识人并不像你们想象中那么枯燥乏味，或者有失准确。如前文所述，也有人说这种方法并非没有危险。正因为如此，中下阶级中的很多人，以及多边形和圆形阶层的所有人，都更喜欢第三种方式。

VI 关于视觉识人的方法

我下面要说的好像与前文不一致。前面我说过在平面国里所有的图形呈现的都是直线形状。如此一来，岂不是无法凭借视觉识别来自不同阶层的人？下面就让我向空间国持怀疑态度的人们解释，我们是如何通过视觉识别人的。

倘若您愿意翻到前文，一定能看到我曾说过触觉识人是一种普遍的方式，但是它只适合在下层社会中使用，而视觉识人只有在上层社会和气候温和的地区才能适用。

我们这种能力之所以在不同地区和不同社会阶层中存在，完全是拜大雾所赐。雾气常年出现于各地，除了热带地区之外。大雾在你们空间国无疑是一种危害，因为它遮蔽风景，令人精神沮丧，还会给人们的健康造成伤害。但是，对我们而言，它却像是空气那样珍贵，宛如我们的艺术女神和智慧源泉。在我继续歌颂它之前，请您听我将它一一道来。

倘若没有大雾，所有直线都将是同样的清晰，无法分辨。在一些不幸的乡村地区，由于空气异常干燥和透明，直线的确是同等清晰。

但是在任何雾气充足的地区，远处的（例如，三英尺之外）物体比两英尺十一英寸之外的物体明显要模糊。因此，只要我们仔细地观察和比较物体之间的清晰度，就可以准确地推算出所看到物体的形状。

与其长篇大论地解释，不如举一个例子。

假如，有两个人朝我走来，我想知道他们的所属阶层。倘若他们是商人或者是医生，换而言之，也就是等边三角形和五边形，那我该如何辨别他们呢？

在空间国里，对于任何略懂几何的小孩而言，这都是非常简单的事情。此时我的视线能将朝我走来的角A一分为二，我的视线正好居于它两条边（即边CA和AB）的中央，而这两条边在我的眼里也是完全同等大小，同等清晰。

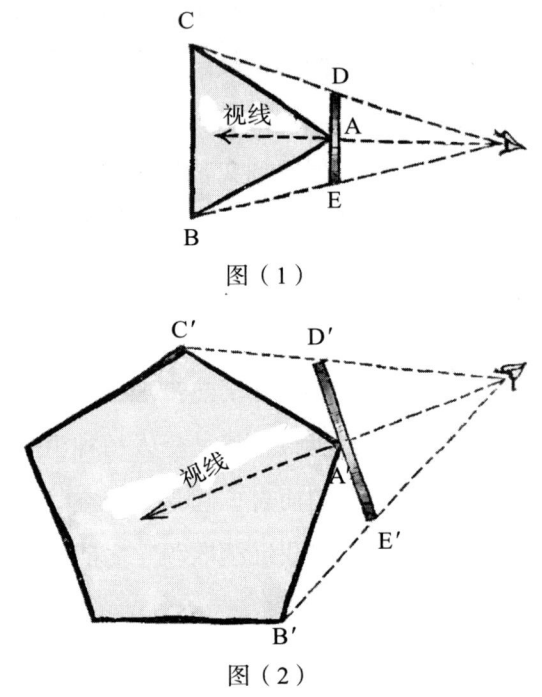

图（1）

图（2）

现在我们再来看图（1）中的商人，我会看见什么情形呢？我看见的是直线DAE，它的中点A会显得异常明亮，因为它离我最近，但是它两边的部分会显得非常暗淡，因为边AC和AB几乎被浓雾遮蔽了，于是看到的商人的远端两个点D和E就显得异常模糊。

我们再来看图（2）中的医生，尽管我看到的也是直线D′A′E′，以及它明亮的中点A′，但是它的两边不会像图（1）那样迅速地变暗淡，因为边A′C′和A′B′是以更平缓的角度隐没在大雾中，因此，我们眼中，医生的两个点D′和E′不会和商人的两点同等模糊。

通过以上两个例子，读者可能会明白，平面国里知识水平较高的阶层，经过长期训练和反复练习，可以凭借目测将中下阶层的人比较准确地区分开来。倘若我空间国的朋友们能掌握这个概念，不觉得我的说法纯属无稽之谈，那我便已达到我的目的。无须过多解释，聪明人一定已经明白其原理。然而缺乏经验的年轻人也许会从我以上的两个例子（这两个例子也适合我辨别我的父亲和儿子）中推断出视觉识人其实异常简单。对这些人而言，我有必要强调，在现实生活中视觉识人存在的很多问题远比他们想象的要微妙和复杂。

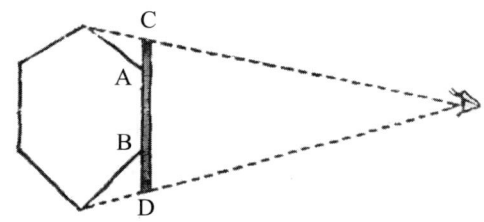

例如，倘若我的三角形父亲朝我走来时，正好是以他的侧边而不是顶角面对我，除非我请他转过身子，或者我绕到他的身旁，否则我会以为他可能是一条直线，换言之，是个女人。同理，当我和我的两个六边形孙子走在一起时，我正面看着他们的一条边AB，结果会和上图所示那样，我会看见他的整个边AB（相对清晰）和两条稍短的边CA和BD（顺着C点和D点的方向逐渐变得暗淡）。

我并不想在此就这个话题做过多的解释。空间国里水平最差的数学家也一定会赞同我以下观点：受过良好教育的图形们有时在移动、旋转、前进或者后退的同时还必须凭借视觉识别移动中社会上层的多边形贵族们（就像在舞厅里或者座谈会上那样），此时他们面对的难题，其实是用来折腾最聪明的学者们的，同时也正好让名声显赫的温特桥大学的几何学教授们有一显身手的机会。君不见，这所大学会定期面向社会中的精英阶层开设视觉识人术等相关课程。

　　然而，只有最富贵的上流社会家庭才有如此充盈的时间和资本去学习这些高雅而昂贵的艺术。我作为一个平庸的数学家，作为一个拥有两个前途无量、形状完全规则的六边形孙子的祖父，发现自己在面对一群旋转的多边形时，也是束手无策。至于普通商人，或者农奴见到这种情形，他们将会和亲爱的读者您一样会变得晕头转向，倘若您是突然被降临到我们平面国。

　　身处这样的人群中，您的四面八方都是笔直的直线，但是他们不同部位的亮度会各有差异。即使你已学完大学三年级的五边形和六边形知识，并且将整门课程的理论背得滚瓜烂熟，你依然会发现自己还需多年的练习，方能在上流社会圈子中交际时不至于冒犯那些名流。请求他们"触摸"你是异常失礼的事情，由于他们极富学识和涵养，因而对你的行为洞若观火，而你对他们却几乎一无所知。总而言之，只有多边形才能在多边形的上流社会中游刃有余。这可是基于我惨痛经历的一点经验之谈。

　　通过习惯养成自然，以及通过避免"触摸"识人而培养出的视觉识人技艺（我称之为本能）令人深感惊讶。好比你们世界里的聋哑人，一旦被允许用手势与人交流，他们就永远无法学会更复杂、但是更有价值的唇读术。他们的手势和唇读如同我们的"触觉"和"视觉"。任何从小过度依赖"触觉"的人都无法完全掌握"视觉"识人术。

　　正因如此，在我们的上流社会中，"触觉"识人是不受鼓励甚至被完全禁止的。他们的儿女从孩提时起，就被送往一流的教会学校，而不是进入公立小学接受触觉教育。在我们那所名声显赫的温特桥大学里，"触觉"识人被视作最严重的违纪，学生如果初犯就会被休学，若再犯将被直接开除。

但是，在下层社会中，视觉识人的技艺却被视作无力享受的奢侈品。普通商人无法负担自己儿子耗费三分之一的人生去学习抽象的知识，因此，穷人的小孩很早就可以凭借"触觉"识人。而多边形阶层的子女接受教育较晚，其中有些小时候看起来甚至发育不良，行动迟缓。与之相比，穷苦人的小孩显得早熟，并且朝气蓬勃。但是等到前者读完大学，开始学以致用的时候，他们的变化简直可谓脱胎换骨。在所有的人文艺术、科学技术领域里，他们都迅速地将三角形竞争对手们远远地甩在身后。

多边形阶层中有极少数人无法通过大学的毕业考试。他们的境遇也异常悲惨。因为他们不但被上层社会拒之门外，而且还会受到下层老百姓的鄙夷。他们既没有学到上流社会本科生和硕士生的系统知识，又没有商人阶层年轻人的成熟与练达。行业协会和政府部门都向他们关闭大门。尽管多数州没有禁止他们结婚，但是事实上他们极难找到合适的配偶。事实表明这些惨遭厄运的人生育的后代即便不是形状不规则，也多半是命运多舛。

但正是从这些被贵族阶层抛弃的可怜虫中，历史上多次产生了革命起义的领袖人物。这些起义影响之大，以致少数富有远见的政客们认为应当严厉镇压这些可怜虫，方法是通过立法判处那些大学毕业考试不及格的人终身监禁，或者以无痛方式处决。

以上涉及违法乱纪这个话题。此事事关重大，我不得不另辟一章。

VII 关于形状不规则的图形

　　前文中我曾做出一个假设：平面国里的每一个人都是规则图形，即长相都很规则，这一切都是上天安排好的。我的意思是：每个妇女都是线条，并且是笔直的直线；工匠和士兵的两条边一定等长；商人的三条边肯定相等；律师（我自己就是其中卑微的一员）四条边长均相等，而且通常每个五边形的所有边线都等长。

　　边线的长度则要取决于每个人的年龄。刚出生的女婴长约一英寸，而身材高挑的女性可能长到一英尺。至于各个阶层的男性，他们所有边线的长度加起来略超三英尺。我们其实并不关心人的边长，而是更看重边长是否相等。稍有头脑的人都能明白，平面国的全部社会生活都基于以下基本事实：即大自然期望我们都拥有等长的边线。

　　由于我们的边长（至少有两条边）都是等长，所以我们只需目测或者稍加触摸就能知道每一个人的内角度数。倘若我们的边不等长，或者说内角度数不均等，我们将不得不通过挨个触摸的方式去辨别每一个角，人生苦短，不容许花费大量时间这样做。如此一来，视觉识人的技艺也将不复存在，触觉识人（暂且也称它为艺术）也将消失，人际交往将变得危险重重甚至根本不可能，人们也不再有信任，对形状也无法做出正确的预见，即使在最简单的社会交往中，大家都会有性命之忧，一言以蔽之，整个文明将重回野蛮状态。

　　您觉得我的这个结论是夸大其词吗？只需稍加思考，您就能从我们的日常生活中找到一个简单例子来证实我们整个社会体制都是建立在人体身形规则的基础之上的。例如，某一天您在路上碰见了两三个人，在瞟了一眼他们暗淡的侧边后，您就立即断定他们是商人，于是邀他们至家中共进午餐。此时您还信心满满，因为大家都知道每个成年三角形占地不过两三平方英寸。但是待您回到家中时，却突然发现其中一个顶角貌似受人尊敬的等边三角形商人，其实是一个对角线长达十二三英寸的平行四边形！天啊，这样一个庞然大物怎么可能进得了你家的大门哦！

　　要是我继续向你啰唆这些在空间国里司空见惯的琐事，那对您的智商简直是一种侮辱。显然，如果图形角度不规则，仅凭一个内角并不足以断定他人身份，而且大家要花一辈子去感觉和揣测自己朋友的身份地位。在人群中如何避免撞上他人本来就已经令学识丰富的正方形头痛不已，要是老天还要让每个图形的角度变得不规则，那么每次聚会必将是一团糟，稍有不慎必定会发生严重受伤事件，倘若里面还有妇女和士兵参与，还很可能还会酿成丧命的悲剧。

　　既然大自然赋予我们规则的体形，适当的做法是依从大自然规律而生活，与之配合。我们这里的"形状不规则"就好比你们空间国里的道德沦丧和犯罪行为，也理应受到相应的惩罚。事实上，我们这儿也不是没有反对者，他们坚持认为形状不规则和道德水平低下之间并不存在必然联系。他们说："形状不规则是与生俱来的，却要受到家人的嘲讽和嫌弃，社会的鄙夷和排挤，还不许参与任何重要的活动。他们出生后的一举一动都受到警察的严密监视，直到他们成年后自己主动接受监督。一旦他们被发现有出格的行为，要么会被判处死刑，要么就是被关在政府机构里担任一个七品小文员。这样一来，他们不但不能结婚，只能以出卖苦力换取一点微薄的收入，而且只能吃住在办公室里，甚至度假时都要受到严密监控。若要这样残酷地对待他们，他们的人性，就算是最纯洁的、最正直的人性，恐怕也会被摧残得面目全非吧！"

　　但是所有这些似是而非的道理都无法让我信服，也无法让我们睿智的政治家相信奉行对不规则形状宽容必定危害国家安全这一公理是我们祖先的失误。毫无疑问，不规则图形的生活是异常艰辛的，但是为了多数人的利益，只能牺牲他们。如果社会允许一个头部长得像三角形的多边形存在，并且任其繁衍出更多不规则的后代，那整个社会岂不是要大乱？难道为了适应这些怪物，我们的房屋，我们的大门，我们的教堂都要进行改建？难道我们看戏或者听讲座时，每个检票员还必须给每个人都测量角度？不规则图形要免除兵役吗？假如是，那该怎样防止他们将低落的情绪传染给他的战友们？再说，他们这些可怜虫肯定也免不了做些坑蒙拐骗的事。试想，一个三角形商人是不是很容易顶着多边形的角冒充多边形，然后跑到商店里大肆购买各种商品！就让那些伪善的慈善家们去呼吁废除不规则图形惩戒条例吧！反正我自己从未见过一个遵纪守法的不规则图形。他们要么虚伪，要么厌世。有的还坏到极点，干着罪恶的勾当。

　　下面，我要介绍一些州郡实施的极端法律。凡是刚出生的婴儿，只要它的内角有任何半度偏差造成的不规则，一律被立即处死。有些天才级别的大师年轻时错误地认为自己的角度偏差了45′，甚至更多。要是他们都英年早逝了，那可是整个国家不可挽回的损失。所幸，我们的医学在压缩、拉伸、钻孔以及包扎手术等方面取得了辉煌的成就，可以部分甚至完全治愈不规则图形。因此，我现在更倾向于采取中庸的办法，不再主张所有的不规则图形必须一律处决。但是如果在他们刚刚成型时，医学委员会就诊断说他们无法治愈，我还是建议采用仁慈的无痛手段处死这些形状不规则的婴儿。

VIII 关于古代的绘画技能

　　要是读者们一直在跟着我的思路，他们肯定不会对平面国的生活略显单调这一说法感到惊讶。当然，我并不是说这里没有战乱纷争、阴谋政变、党派之争，以及其他各种让历史变得有趣的社会现象，我也并不否认对人生的疑惑与数学难题奇妙地交织在一起，总是能诱导人们去探索和争论，也给我们的生活平添了许多你们空间国里难以想象的乐趣。但是，从美学和艺术的角度来看，我们的生活确实单调，非常单调。

　　既然平面国里所有自然风光，所有文物古迹，所有肖像画，所有花朵，甚至所有的生命，都是一条线段，除了明暗度的差异之外没有任何区别，那我还能用别的什么词语来形容我们的生活呢？

　　我们的世界也并非一直如此。我们的历史曾记载，色彩曾给我们先辈的生活带来过乐趣，这一段历史维持了六百多年。当时有一位先人（是一位五边形，关于他的姓名有多种不同的说法）意外地发现了单色的基本构成，并且掌握了基本的绘画技巧。据说他先给自己的房屋装扮了色彩，然后又给奴隶以及他的父亲、儿子和孙子们，最后还给他自己也涂上颜色。这种装饰方便又漂亮，因而获得大家的青睐。无论这位色彩学家（最权威的大人物们都不约而同地这样称呼他）在哪里改变自己外形的颜色，都会引起注意，并受到尊敬。于是，大家都不用再"触摸"他，也不会将他的前面和后背弄混淆。他的邻居们不需要通过任何计算便能知道他的所有行为动作，没有人会撞到他，所有人都为他让道，而在拥挤的人群中我们这些没有色彩的正方形和五边形只有用尽全力大声吆喝才能通行，而他却不用发出任何声音。

　　他的创新之举像野火一般，迅速蔓延开来。一个星期后，他所在区的每个正方形和三角形都模仿了这位色彩学家的做法，只有几个保守的五边形还在死守传统。一两个月后，甚至十二边形们都在使用这个创新发明。一年之后，这一创举就传遍了全国除了最顶层的上流社会之外的每一个阶层。很自然，这个方法很快从色彩学家的所在区域传播到了周边地区。经过两代人的繁衍，平面国里所有的图形都有了色彩，只有女性和牧师群体除外。

　　老天似乎在这里设置了一道障碍，防止将以上发明传播到这两个群体。拥有多条边是色彩创新的前提条件。"上天以边数之差暗示色彩之别"，这是那个年代里口口相传的真理，结果将整个城镇改变。显然，这一说法对我们的牧师和女性并不适用。由于后者只有一条边，因此，就数量上和数理上而言，其实是没有边。而由于只有边线长度，即周长，前者（倘若自认为自己完全属于圆形阶层，而不是长着很多短边的高级多边形）总是惯于自诩自己也没有边（这又是女性们承认且深感遗憾的）。因此，就造成了这两个群体不受"边数之差暗示色彩之别"公理约束的现象，于是当其他所有人都禁不住给自己涂上色彩的诱惑时，只有牧师和女性依然保持着纯洁的本色，没有受到色彩污染。

　　不道德，放荡不羁，目无纪律，毫不科学，无论你用什么字眼形容，从美学角度来看，历史上色彩革命的那一段时间是平面国艺术发展史的辉煌童年时代。只可惜，这个童年时代从未进入成熟的壮年期，甚至没有进入少年。然而，能够生活在那个年代就已然是一种幸福，因为活着就意味着可以看得见。即使是在小型的聚会上观察人群也是一件令人愉悦的事情。据说，我们最有学问的老师和最有经验的演员不止一次被教堂或者剧院里人群的色彩绚丽的服装弄得晕头转向。但是，场面最壮观的却莫过于盛大的阅兵大典。

两万个等腰三角形士兵组成的列队突然转身，他们底边的漆黑色就瞬间变为两边的橙色或者紫色；等边三角形民兵组成的方阵身着红、白、蓝三色军服；身穿淡紫、深蓝、橙黄以及焦土色军装的正方形炮兵们在朱红色的大炮旁迅速换位；此时身披五种色彩绚丽颜色的五边形和六种色彩的六边形全速通过，他们是外科医生、几何学者以及侍从武官——所有这些蔚为壮观的阅兵盛况都足以让人对下面的故事深信不疑：由于被自己统帅的部队多彩斑斓的服装完全迷倒，一位战功卓越的圆形元帅将自己的指挥棒和绣有皇冠的肩章扔至地上，大声宣布说要用它们换取艺术家手里的画笔。我们还依稀能从当时丰富的语言和词汇中管窥那一段辉煌的历史以及它的美学成就。

色彩革命时期最普通的人使用的最普通的话语里都充满着富有色彩气息的语言和思想。时至今日，我们依然要感谢那个年代，因为我们今天最优美的诗歌和学术语言中的所有韵律都得益于此。

IX 关于普遍使用色彩的法案

由于没有人再需要视觉识人术，因而大家也就不再使用它。于是，几何学、静力学、动力学以及其他相关课程也被人们认为是多余的知识，并且在大学里变得默默无闻，无人问津。很快，更低层次的触觉识人术在小学里也遭遇了同样的厄运。而后，由于等腰三角形阶层认为小学也不再需要使用三角形样本，而且还拒绝从罪犯阶层里挑选样本送入教育服务领域，从而导致整个等腰三角形阶层的人口数与日俱增并且素质也变得每况愈下，因为现在他们不需要像以前一样被送进教育机构，以驯化他们的粗野禀性，以及达到降低他们人口数量的目的。

由于士兵和工匠们已上升到和最高级的多边形阶层平等的地位，并且只需凭借色彩识人术就可以解决所有的困难和生活问题，无论是静力学的还是动力学方面的，所以他们渐渐坚定地认为（也的确有道理）：他们与多边形阶层之间没有很大的差别。出于对视觉识人术陷入无人问津的地步感到不满，他们开始大胆地要求法律禁止所有"被贵族垄断的技艺"，并且取消所有资助视觉识人术以及数学和触觉的研究基金。不久以后，他们又开始主张，既然色彩已经是所有图形的第二属性，并且它也消除了阶级差别，那么法律就应当一视同仁，让每一个个体和阶层都享有绝对平等地位和同等权利。

当革命领袖们发现上层阶级对此犹豫不决时，他们又进一步增加了革命诉求。他们的基本主张是要求所有阶级，包括牧师和妇女在内，都应当装饰色彩，以表达对色彩的敬意。当有人反对说牧师和妇女没有边时，他们辩称老天爷已降旨要让每一个人的前半身（也就是指长着眼睛和嘴唇的部分）和后半身有所区别。据此，他们在一次规模空前的平面国全国代表大会上提交了一份提案，建议每位妇女长着眼睛和嘴巴的前半身装扮上红色，另一部分则扮成绿色。（近乎圆形的）牧师也应如此，以眼睛和嘴巴为两个端点的前半圆扮成红色，后半圆则扮成绿色。

然而，这一提案中暗藏着不少玄机。它绝不是由任何等腰三角形提出来的，因为他们地位低下，思维简单，更甭提有什么治国之道。这一提案其实是由一个不规则的圆形提出来的。他童年时本应被处死，但是却被愚蠢的当局者特赦了，现在他注定要让这个国家战火纷飞，生灵涂炭。

这个提案的第一个目的是要让各个阶层的妇女们转而倒向色彩革新派。因为，通过立法让妇女和牧师穿上相同的两种色彩，革命分子就可以确保每一个妇女从特定角度看起来和牧师一模一样，从而让她们获得同等的尊重。显然，这一提案深深打动了广大妇女阶层的心。

有些读者可能还心存疑惑，牧师怎么可能和妇女看起来一模一样呢？还是让我来简单解释一下吧。

假设一位妇女按照新的法令穿着打扮，即前半身（长着眼睛和嘴巴的部分）扮成红色，而后半身穿成绿色。当你从她的侧面看过去，显然她是一条一半红、一半绿的直线。

我们再假设一位牧师（见下图），他的嘴巴为M点，前半圆AMB穿成红色，后半圆为绿色，这样一来他的直径AB就正好将整个圆分成红色和绿色的两半。倘若你凝视这位德高望重的牧师时，视线正好处在他的直径AB线上，那么你看到的就是直线CBD，其中一半CB是红色，另一半BD为绿色。整个线段CD可能比成年妇女的长度要短，并且他的颜色朝着线段两端淡化得更快。但是由于两种色彩会立刻让你想到它们所代表的身份（即使不是社会阶层），因而你会很容易忽视其他细节。一方面你会很清楚地记得由于视觉识人术在色彩革命时代给社会造成了危害，因而这种方法早已被废除，另一方面我们几乎可以肯定妇女们会迅速学会如何将自己的颜色朝两端淡化，以便冒充圆形阶层。如此一来，我亲爱的读者，您一定明白了其实色彩法案已将我们陷入了由牧师和妇女外形容易混淆带来的巨大危险之中。

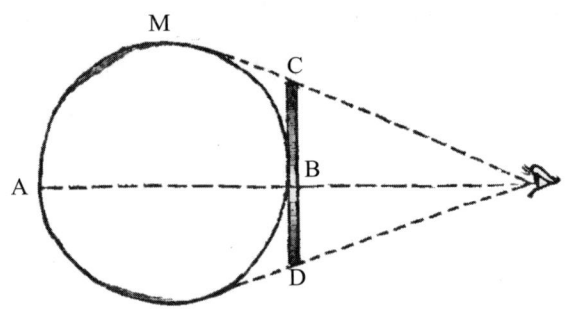

我们很容易想象得到脆弱的妇女阶层是如何醉心于这一愿景的。她们热切地盼望着即将到来的这种身份混乱状况。

如此一来，她们就可能在家里听到，并非针对自己而是针对她们丈夫和兄弟的政治和宗教秘密，她们甚至可能以牧师阶层的名义发号施令。在户外，由于没有任何其他颜色，只有红绿两色，民众肯定会被误导犯下大量的错误，而妇女们将在路人的注目礼中获得圆形阶层失去的尊贵。就算妇女们做出的各种轻佻和出格地行为都将转嫁到圆形阶层身上，并且让后者承受恶名，就算整个社会结构都将因此被颠覆，她们也将不为所动。甚至圆形阶层的妇女也一致赞成普遍实施色彩法案。

这一法案的第二个目的就是要逐步瓦解圆形阶层的道德优越感。在以前社会大众智力普遍底下的年代，圆形阶层尚且能够保持自己的高贵和优雅。由于从孩提时代起，贵族阶层就在家里适应了没有色彩的环境，所以他们一直对神圣的、只有经过智力训练才能学会的视觉识人术抱残守缺。甚至，到了普遍实施色彩法案通过的日子，他们还在坚守传统，并且还摆出一副绝不与大众同流合污的态度，以显示他们高高在上的优越感。

时过境迁，我前文说到的那个奸诈的不规则圆形（即这条恶毒法案的真实发起人）突然坚决要求通过强迫圆形阶层接受色彩污染，以达到降低他们社会地位的目的。同时还以剥夺他们纯洁而无色的住房的方式，杜绝他们在家中训练视觉识人术，从而降低他们的智力。一旦受到色彩的污染，每一个圆形，无论老少，都免不了互相攻击。只有在分辨父母的时候，圆形阶层家庭的婴儿才会遇到色彩识人带来的困难。这通常是由于母亲外表看起来太像男性，导致婴儿无法建立起对两性的正常认知。如此一来，牧师阶层的智力优势就消失殆尽了，随之而来的是贵族阶层立法机构和特权阶级的土崩瓦解。

X 关于镇压色彩革命

普遍实施色彩法案引发的动荡持续了三年，直到它快要结束的最后一刻，煽动骚乱的人似乎还胜券在握。

此前，多边形已被沦为士兵，并且组建了一支军队，但是还是被强大的等腰三角形彻底消灭了，而此时正方形和五边形却一直在袖手旁观。更糟糕的是，一些最优秀的圆形领袖却成了夫妻同室操戈的牺牲品。在政治仇恨的煽动下，很多贵族家庭的妻子们在丈夫们面前喋喋不休地恳求他们放弃反对色彩法案，其中一些人在恳求无果的情况下，竟然开始袭击并杀害自己无辜的孩子和丈夫，最终也葬送了自己的性命。据记载，在那场持续三年的动乱中，至少有二十三个圆形贵族死于夫妻斗殴。

整个贵族阶层都危在旦夕。牧师们除了投降或者被消灭之外，似乎毫无选择。而就在此时，一件离奇的小事，却让整个社会形势风云突变。现在看来，政治家们绝不应当忽视，而应当期待，甚至有时还应亲自策划这样的偶然事件，因为他们具有煽动民众情感的超强能力。

事件起源于一个身份卑微、头脑简单的等腰三角形，他的顶角不超过4°。在某一次掠夺了一位商人的商铺后，他偶然摆弄起了商人的色彩。于是他给自己装扮上了十二面体的十二种不同颜色（另一种说法是他是被迫的）。有一回他在街上勾搭上了一位多边形贵族的女儿，她刚失去了双亲。以前他曾追求过这位少女，但是并未成功。这次在他各种花言巧语的攻势下，加上又有很多的巧合事件发生，以及她那些亲戚过于愚蠢和粗心大意，他最终成功地俘获这位可怜新娘的芳心。可是，这位伤心的姑娘一发现自己上当受骗，便立刻自尽了。

于是这桩惨剧在全国传得沸沸扬扬，而全国妇女们的情感也很快就被煽动起来了。她们一方面很同情这位死去的姑娘，另一方面还担心自己以及自己的姐妹和女儿也可能是上当受骗了，因而她们对色彩法案的立场也完全发生了转变。于是，很多妇女公开宣称自己反对该法案，而其他的人只需要稍加刺激就会同样转变立场。圆形阶层抓住这个有利的时机，迅速召集了全国代表大会。他们不但允许由犯人担任保安人员，而且还让大量反对色彩革命的妇女出席这次大会。

在这次盛况空前的集会上，有一位圆形阶层的首领，名叫潘多塞克拉斯。他发现现场的十二万等腰三角形对他发出集体抗议。但是在他宣布圆形阶层将采取妥协的政策之后，等腰三角形们终于安静了下来。他说圆形阶层准备服从大多数人的意见，并且接受色彩法案。于是抗议声就变成了掌声，他还邀请那位色彩学家，即这次骚乱的领袖，进入议会大厅，代表他的所有追随者，接受统治阶层的投降。接下来他还发表了一份堪称修辞学典范的演讲。这篇演讲几乎持续了一整天，其主要意思冗长得简直无法概括。

这位首领用庄严肃穆的语气说道，既然他们现在致力于改革和创新，那么就有必要对整个议案进行最后一次讨论。讨论内容既要包括其优点，也应包含它的缺陷。他有意无意地提到该法案对商人、专业人士阶层以及绅士阶层造成的威胁。此时虽然等腰三角形们又开始窃窃私语，但是他宣称尽管该法案有各种缺陷，只要大多数代表通过，他还是愿意接受它。于是，等腰三角形们才再次安静了下来。然而，此时显然除了等腰三角形之外，所有其他阶层都已受到圆形首领言论的影响，他们要么中立，要么开始反对该法案。

接下来，该首领又转向工人阶层。他坚称他们的利益绝不应当被忽视，但是如果他们打算接受色彩法案，那他们至少应当通盘考虑一下该法案的后果。他说，本来有很多工人很快就能进入规则三角形阶层，还有一些人马上就能见到自己的小孩获得一份自己无法企及的荣誉。但是这些荣誉将肯定无法兑现。因为，一旦全面通过色彩法案，所有的荣誉都将被取消；规则图形将和不规则图形之间不再有任何差别；各阶层不但不会进步，反而会倒退；只需经过几代人繁衍的时间，工人就会被堕落到士兵阶层，甚至是犯人阶层；政治权利将会落入人口最多的阶层，即罪犯阶层。他们的人口数量已经超越工人阶层，并且一旦自然补偿法则被破坏，他们的数量将很快超过所有其他阶层人数的总和。

此时，工匠阶层开始低声附和圆形首领，而那位色彩学家听后，不禁大惊失色，他试图站起来反驳。然而他早已陷入卫兵的包围之中，因而不得不保持沉默。接下来，那位圆形首领又开始煽动妇女们。他厉声说道，要是色彩法案获得通过，所有的婚姻将无法获得法律保障，所有妇女获得的荣誉也会失去保证；每个家庭里将充斥着欺骗与虚伪。最后，他哭丧着脸说道，而比这更快降临的"将是死亡"。

谁知，最后那句话竟然是他们密谋好的行动暗号。只见他话音未落，等腰三角形中的犯人们就冲上前来，立刻刺死了那位可怜的色彩学家。旋即，规则图形阶层闪开了一条道路，让一队妇女在圆形贵族们的引导下转过身子开始攻击尚未反应过来的士兵们。而工匠们，则效仿起规则图形，只是束手旁观。另外一大群犯人则早已将各个出入口包围得水泄不通。

就这样，战斗演变成了一边倒的杀戮，因而并没有持续太久。在圆形贵族娴熟的指挥下，几乎每一个妇女都变成了致命杀手。她们很多人直接将敌人一击致命，自己却毫发无损。而对面的等腰三角形却陷入了群龙无首的混乱状态，他们腹背受敌，前面遭到隐身妇女的攻击，后面又被犯人切断了退路。不一会儿，他们就乱作一团，嘴里还大喊着"叛徒，叛徒！"而正是这句话才彻底葬送了他们自己的性命。因为，每个等腰三角形误以为对方说自己是叛徒，于是开始互相攻击。就这样，还没有等到那些妇女发起第二次进攻，他们就开始自相残杀起来。不到半个小时，人数众多的等腰三角形就被消灭得一干二净。此次战斗中，共计有一万四千个违法作乱份子死于自己人的锐角之下。他们的生命终于换回了往日的宁静。

圆形阶层则马不停蹄地继续扩大自己的战果。他们虽然赦免了工人阶层，但是却大幅削减了他们的数量。此外，他们很快组建了等边三角形民兵队，而且规定只要理由恰当，无须经过社会委员会的严格审查，每个疑似不规则图形都可以由军事法庭直接判处死刑。士兵和工匠家庭则面临为期超过一年的随机检查，在此期间，在任何城市和乡镇，村庄和村落里，只要发现因没有被送到学校或者大学里作为样本从事教育服务，或者因为违反平面国人口构成自然法则而多出的底层人口，将一律被清除。

毋庸置疑，此后色彩就被彻底废除，而拥有色彩也被绝对禁止。除了圆形阶层和有资质的科学教师之外，任何人如果使用了表示颜色的词语，都将面临严惩。只有在对最尊贵和最神秘的阶层开放的大学里，只有在解释深奥的数学问题时，他们才被准许使用少量的色彩词汇。因为我自己从未有幸进入过如此高级的学府，所以这些也只是我的听闻。

而在平面国里其他地方，色彩早已消失得无影无踪。世界上仅有一个人掌握着制造色彩的秘方，他就是现任的圆形首领。只有等到他临终前躺在病榻上，才会将这一秘方传授给另外一人——他的继任者。这也是该秘方留传的唯一方法。为了避免它被泄露，平面国每年都会处决一批工人，然后由另外一批新手弥补他们的空缺。时至今日，当贵族们自己回顾起当年由色彩法案引发的那场社会动乱时，也不禁骇然失色。

XI 关于我们的牧师

现在，我得结束对平面国概况的赘述，以转入本书的重点，即启发人们对神秘空间的探索。这才是本书的宗旨所在。前面章节权当序言。

正因如此，我必须省略很多对现象的细节描写，但是我敢自信地说，我的读者们对这些现象产生的原因肯定兴趣盎然。比如，没有腿脚，我们是如何做到迈步和停步的？没有双手，我们是如何用木头、石块以及砖头搭起建筑的？在没有横向压力的情况下，我们又是如何打地基的？再例如，我们平面国的雨水又是如何每间隔一段时间在不同地区降落，从而保证北方地区不会拦截本应降落在南方的降水？我们的高山、矿藏、树木、蔬菜是什么属性？而我们的四个季节和庄家收割又是什么情形？我们的字母表以及书写系统是如何适应直线型便签的？还有其他成千上万个生活细节，我都不得不省略。在此，我只想提醒我的读者，我这样做并不是因为我忘记交代它们，而是为了节约您宝贵的阅读时间。

然而，在进入本书的主题之前，毫无疑问读者们还会希望我再对平面国社会的中流砥柱们简单描述一番。因为他们既是我们行为规范的制定者、命运的掌控人，也是我们敬仰和尊崇的对象。毋庸置疑，他们就是圆形阶层，或者说牧师阶层。

我虽称他们为牧师，但是他们的工作并不仅仅限于该名称字面所包含的范围。对于我们而言，牧师就是所有商务、艺术以及科学的掌门人，他们是贸易通商、政治军队、建筑工程、文化教育、法律道德以及宗教界的统管者。他们是所有事务的缘起，但是又不参与任何具体工作，一切事务都自有他人办理。

尽管普通大众将每一个称为圆形的图形都视作圆形，但是教育程度较高的阶层都知道圆形其实并非真正的圆形，他们只是拥有很多条边的多边形。因而他们的边数越多，就越像圆形。当一个多边形的边数变得异常大的时候，例如三百或者四百，即使最精确的触觉识人术也难以分辨出其内角度数。其实，真正的难点还不在于此，而在于正如我前面所说的，上层社会根本就不学触觉识人术，因为通过触摸识别圆形被认为是对他们极大的侮辱。上层社会拒绝使用触觉的这种习惯，正好给圆形阶层蒙上了一层神秘的面纱。于是他们从小就开始刻意隐瞒自己的边数。因为多边形的周长平均为三英尺，所以，一个拥有三百条边的多边形的每一条边长都不会超过百分之一英尺，换而言之，就是十分之一英寸。而一个拥有六百或者七百条边的多边形的每条边长就只有空间国里一个针头那么宽。而为了表达敬意，人们都宣称当世的圆形首领拥有一万条边。

依照自然法则的规定，规则图形的下一代都会比自己多一条边，然而圆形阶层后代晋升的规则却不受此法则约束。倘若这个规则适用于所有阶层，那么圆形阶层的边数就仅仅是一个纯粹的数学问题，而等边三角形的第四百九十七代子孙也一定会是拥有五百条边的多边形。但是事实并非如此。老天爷对圆形阶层的繁衍做出了两条极其苛刻的规定。其一，他们到达的阶级层次越高，其发展速度就变得越快；其二，他们发展的速度越快，出现不孕不育的概率也会变得越大。因此，很少拥有四百或者五百条边的多边形家庭能生育儿子，而能生育两个或者更多儿子的家庭则根本没有出现过。事实上，拥有五百条边的多边形生育的儿子可能有五百五十甚至六百条边。

医学技术在上层阶级的进化中也起到了积极的作用。我们的医生已发现上层阶级多边形婴儿的娇小而脆弱的侧边可以做折断手术，因而他们可以精确地重塑他的外形。例如，一个拥有两百或者三百条边的多边形有时候（绝非总是如此，因为断边手术有极大的风险）会通过手术折断自己子女的边，从而让子女直接跨越两百甚至三百代。如此一来，他们的边数就会翻了一番，仿佛地位也会变得更加尊贵。

大量前途光明的小孩做了这种手术的实验品，而其中又只有百分之一的幸运儿能活下来。但是那些处于圆形阶层边缘的多边形父母们对这种手术却依然趋之若鹜，以至于在这些贵族父母中，没有哪一个不是在自己的长子尚未满月之时，就将他送至医院去的。

他们的成败取决于随后的一年。这一年过后，绝大多数小孩的结局都是给医院的墓地增添一座墓碑，如果偶尔有一个幸存活了下来，则会有盛大的游行队伍将这个幸运儿送回至他欣喜若狂的父母家中。他将不再是多边形，而是圆形（至少礼仪上是如此）。这种幸运的故事又诱导了无数的多边形父母义无反顾地牺牲自己的小孩。

XII 关于我们牧师的教条

圆形阶层的教条可以简要地用以下箴言概括，即"外形决定一切"。无论是政治、宗教还是道德的所有教条都是以改善个人和集体的外形为目标——即上升为圆形阶层，其他所有目的都居于次要地位。

圆形阶层的功绩之一是镇压了自古就有的那些歪理邪说。在这些歪理的蛊惑下，人们盲目地相信人的命运由意志力、勤奋、训练、鼓励和赞美决定，而绝非什么外形决定。正是我前面提到的那位潘多塞克拉斯，即色彩革命的平息者，让人类坚信外形决定人的一生。假如你出生在一个形状不规则的等腰三角形家庭，除非你去等腰三角形医院做外形矫正手术，否则你就注定命运坎坷。同理，倘若你是一个外形不规则的三角形、正方形或者多边形，你必须要去整形医院矫正自己的外形，否则你将来不是蹲监狱就是死于国家级刽子手的锐角之下。

这位潘多塞克拉斯将所有的行为过错（包括最轻微的行为失当和最恶劣的犯罪）归咎于身体外形偏差。导致这些偏差的原因可能是在人群中发生了碰撞、疏于身体锻炼或者锻炼过度，甚至是由于气温骤变而导致了身体脆弱部位的萎缩或者臃肿。因此，这位杰出的哲学家得出的结论是，严格讲来，善恶之行都不应当是褒扬和批评的对象。比如说，当一个正方形坚定地维护客户的利益时，你应该仰慕他的标准外形，而不是赞扬他的正直行为；你应当谴责等腰三角形那无可救药的两条不等长的腰，而不是批评他的撒谎和偷盗行为。

　　理论上来讲，这一教义无可非议，但是在实践中，它却有诸多弊病。当一个等腰三角形无赖狡辩说，他是由于自己外形不规则才忍不住去偷窃，此时，作为一个地方法官，如果你回答说，正因如此他才控制不住自己去骚扰邻居，那么，你就无法判处他死刑，整个案件也就到此结束了。然而，由于死刑不适用于处理家庭纠纷，因此，外形决定命运的理论有时就会陷入自相矛盾。我不得不承认，有时我自己的某个六边形孙子恳请我的原谅时，也辩解说是气温骤变导致他身体不适，然后他才变得不听话的。我也承认，我不应该责怪他，而应怪罪他的外形。然而只有通过多吃高级糖果才能改善外形。这样一来，我既无法从逻辑上否定，又不能事实上肯定他的说法。

　　因此，我认为适当的批评和惩戒对我孙子的外形可以产生潜在的积极影响，尽管我承认这种猜测并没有任何依据。其实，也并不只有我一个人采用这一策略处理这种两难问题。我发现很多担任出庭法官的圆形贵族，在法庭上一边褒扬规则图形，另一边也责备不规则图形，我也亲眼看过他们在家里批评子女时，会大声说"对"和"错"这样的字眼，仿佛他们相信这些词语是真的客观存在，而且人类真的能够分辨是非。

　　通过不断地给人们灌输外形决定一切的观念，圆形阶层完全颠倒了空间国里父子之间的伦理道德。在你们空间国里，子女理应尊敬父母，但是对于我们（圆形阶层除外，因为他们是大家敬仰的主要对象）而言，恰恰相反，每个人应当尊重他的孙子，要是他没有孙子，就尊重儿子。但是，我们的"尊重"绝不是"溺爱"的意思，而是服从家族最高利益。圆形阶层教诲大家说，父亲的职责就是服从自己子嗣的利益，只有这样他们才能够增加全社会以及自己子女的福祉。

　　如果一个身份卑微的正方形可以斗胆指出圆形阶层的一丁点不足之处，那么我觉得，从圆形阶层与妇女的关系中就可以看出其思想体系的弱点。

由于反对生育不规则婴儿这一点对社会的发展至关重要，因而凡是有身形不规则家族史的妇女都不适合嫁给那些决心要让自己的子孙后代逐步进入上流社会的男子。

男性图形的不规则程度只需测量即可获知，然而由于所有妇女看起来都是规则的直线，所以我们不得不通过其他方式了解她们那潜在的不规则性，即她们可能给后代造成的潜在影响。而这种潜在影响只能从政府严密保管的家族系谱中了解到。要是一位妇女的家谱没有获得政府认证，那她就会被禁止结婚。

大家可能以为圆形阶层一定比任何其他阶层更想挑选一位没有任何污点的妻子，因为他们有很强的家族荣誉感，也非常渴望生育一个将来可能成为圆形首领的后嗣。但是事实并非如此。似乎社会等级越高，人们对是否娶规则图形为妻的在意程度反而越低。然而，对于雄心勃勃的等腰三角形阶层而言，任何事情都无法诱惑他们娶一位有不规则家族史的妇女为妻，因为他们毫无例外都希望自己生出一个等边三角形儿子。正方形和五边形，由于相信自己的家族一直处于进步之中，不会去过多了解自己第五百代子孙的情况；而六边形或者十二边形就更不关心妻子的血统了。也曾有一位圆形成员自愿娶了一位曾祖父是不规则图形的女子为妻，其原因可能是女方家的身世更为显赫，也可能是她拥有一副迷人的低沉嗓音。我们比你们更认为，这样的嗓音是难得一见的"优良妇德"。

正如人们预料的那样，这种门不当、户不对的夫妻要么就是生出不规则但无害的、或者边数更少的子女，要么就是根本无法生育。但是这些恶果并不足以阻止其他人继续效仿他们。上层社会的多边形损失一两条边不会轻易被别人发现，再说他们也可以通过前文提到的新型矫形手术而弥补上那几条边。此外，由于圆形阶级处于上等阶层，他们一般对自己无法生育的情况会保守秘密。但是，如果这种丑行不被阻止，那么圆形阶层人口萎缩进程很快会加速，直到不久的将来，他们再也无法生育出担任圆形首领的后代。到那时，整个平面国的社会将土崩瓦解。

此外还有一条警告正在我耳边回响，我也很难提出它的解决方案。这条警告也和我们与妇女的关系有关。大约三百年前，当时的圆形首领就颁布法令规定，鉴于妇女感性有余而理性不足，她们既不应当被继续视作具有理性的人，也不应当再接受情感教育。于是她们不再学习阅读，甚至还没有掌握如何计算自己丈夫和子女内角数的心算法。结果导致她们的智力一代不如一代。这种妇女不受教育的政策，或者说无为主义，时至今日依然盛行。

我所担心的是，尽管这一政策的出发点无比正确，但是事实上它却给男性造成了很大伤害。

这一政策造成的结果是我们这些男性不得不使用两套语言，甚至使用两种情感。面对女性时，我们会使用"爱情""责任""正确""错误""遗憾""希望"等词语，以及其他一些缺乏理性的情感词语。而这些词语代表的概念根本就不存在，我们编造这些词语的唯一目的不过是不想让女性变得过于强大。但是，在我们男性之间，在我们的书籍里，我们却会使用另一套完全不同的词汇，也即我所说的术语。于是，"爱情"就变成了"对利益的期盼"，"责任"则变成了"必然性"或者"适当性"，还有其他一些词语也被相应的转换。不仅如此，在女性面前，我们使用的语言都饱含着对她们的无比尊重，而且她们也相信我们对她们的爱慕之情并不少于我们对圆形首领的敬畏之心。但是，在她们的背后，除了小孩以外，没有人不说她们是一群"没有头脑的动物"。

我们在有女性参与的会议上宣扬的宗教信仰和在他处所说的也截

然不同。

　　这样一来，我又开始担忧我们语言与思想上的两套做法会给青少年带来沉重的负担，尤其是当他们还只有三岁的时候，一边要脱离母亲的照料并学习如何抛弃妈妈教的词语，另一边还要开始学习科学的词汇和术语。三百年前，我们祖先是何等的睿智，相比之下，我们的数学能力又是何等的低下。且不说，倘若一位妇女偷偷学习阅读后将自己的所学传授给同伴，那该是多么危险，更甭提有些不听话的小孩还可能会无意间向他们的母亲们透露出父亲背地里使用的那一套语言。仅凭这种两套做法就会降低男性智力这一条，我也要呼吁最高领导层重新调整妇女教育政策。

第二部分　其他世界

"啊，美丽的新世界！
有这么多出色的人物！"[1]

[1] 出自英国伟大剧作家威廉·莎士比亚戏剧《暴风雨》。——译者注

I　我是如何看见直线国的

　　那是我们世代的一九九九年的倒数第二日，也是漫长假期的第一天。我整日都沉浸在挚爱的几何学研究中，直到晚上休息时，脑海里还萦绕着一道数学难题。于是，我做了一个梦。

　　在梦里，我看见一大群很短的直线（起初我以为是妇女），中间散布有一些更细小的发光点。他们在同一条直线上来来回回移动。据我目测，他们的移动速度完全一致。

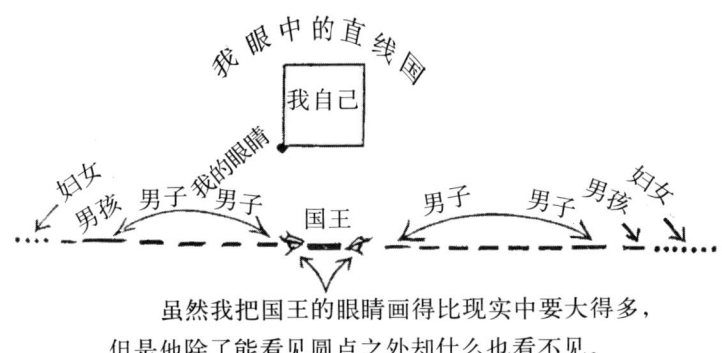

虽然我把国王的眼睛画得比现实中要大得多，
但是他除了能看见圆点之外却什么也看不见。

　　他们一边走动，一边发出一些让人无法听懂的叽叽喳喳声。有时，他们会突然停止移动，然后又陷入一片寂静。

　　我走到一位看起来像妇女的直线跟前，和她打招呼，但是对方却毫无反应。于是我又试了两次，可是依然没有回应。由于实在无法再忍受这种无礼行为，我只好先直接将自己的嘴巴凑到她的跟前，将她逼停，然后大声地问道："女士，你们聚会时，为什么要发出这些含混不清的叽叽喳喳声？为什么还要在同一条直线上来来回回走动？"

"我并非女性，"这条直线答道，"朕乃本国之君主。你，为何要入侵朕的直线国？"听到这意外的回答，我赶紧乞求他宽恕自己的冒昧之举。我说自己是一个外地人，并恳求他向我介绍一番他的王国。但是我很难获得自己感兴趣的信息，因为这位国王以为我早已熟知这一切，我只不过是在假装无知，和他开玩笑罢了。但是，经过穷追不舍的提问，我还是打听到了以下情况：

似乎这位可怜而又无知的君主（这个头衔是他自封的）一直相信这条他称之为自己的王国、并从未曾离开过的直线就是整个世界，也即整个空间。在他的直线王国之外，他既无法动弹也看不见，因此他对直线之外的任何事物都一无所知。我第一次和他打招呼的时候，虽然他听到了我的声音，但是由于这个声音异常奇怪，所以他就没有搭理。他说："未见其人，只闻其声，它仿佛是从我的身体里面发出的。"在我将嘴巴凑近他的世界之前，他根本无法看见我，只能听到一团含混的声音冲击着他的外边（而他却称之为内脏）。在他的世界或者说这条直线之外，一切都是空白。哦不，还不能说是空白，因为空白的意思是空间，因而只能说是虚无。

他的臣民包括那些小小线段的男性和圆点女性，他们的行动和视线都只能限制在自己的世界之内，也即那条直线之内。无须解释，在他们的视野范围之内，能看到的除了一个个圆点之外，别无他物。在直线国居民眼里，男人、女人、小孩以及一切物体都是圆点。只有凭借声音，他们才能区分性别和年龄。另外，由于每个人都占据了他们国家那条狭窄的直线道路，因此没有人能够通过左右移动给别人让道。于是，直线国居民走路时，都不能超越他人。这意味着，一旦为邻，终身为邻。他们国家的邻里关系就像我们的夫妻，直到死时才能结束。

满眼都是圆点，行动又不能超出那条直线，这样的生活对我来

说简直是悲惨至极。但是我很奇怪，为何这位国王却过得如此神采飞
扬，逍遥自在。在建立家庭关系异常艰难的生存环境下，直线国的居
民是如何享受鱼水之欢的呢？虽然这个问题难以启齿，但是在犹豫了
一会儿之后，我还是忍不住打听起国王的私生活。"我的妃子和皇子
们，"他回答道，"都非常健康和快乐。"

　　我对他的回答将信将疑，因为我在进入直线国之前做的梦里就注
意到紧贴着国王的无一例外都是男性。于是我贸然接话道："请您恕
罪，但是我实在无法想象在您和妻子们之间隔着那么多外人，又不能
绕过他们的情况下，您是如何接近她们的呢？难道说在直线国里，婚
姻和生育儿女可以不需要两性结合？"

　　"你怎么能问如此荒唐的问题呢？"国王回答道，"倘若真如你
所言，我国人口岂不是很快就会灭绝？事实绝非你说的那般，邻居关
系并非就是秦晋之好。养育后代事关重大，绝不可能依赖这种随机的
邻里关系。这一点你也很清楚。既然你喜欢装作无知，那朕就当你是
直线国里最不懂事的小孩。现在我要正告你，我们的琴瑟之和是以声
音和听觉来完成的。"

　　"显然，你已经注意到我的每个子民都有两个嘴巴，或者说两幅
嗓音，还有两只眼睛。两个嘴巴分别处于他线段的两头，一头发出男
低音，另一头发出男高音。我很抱歉地告诉你，我和你说话的时候其
实无法分辨出你的高低音。"于是，我回答说自己只有一副嗓音，并
告诉他我也没有发现他有两个声音。"这更加证实了我的推测，"国
王说道，"你不是男性，而是一个低音受损的女子，并且耳朵也完全
不管用。让我接着说。"

　　"老天安排每一个男人必须娶两个妻子——"

　　"为什么是两个？"我问道。

　　"你装得有点过头了。"他大喊道。

"如果不做到高低音搭配，天下怎么可能有幸福美满的夫妻呢？如果男人的高音和低音没有两个女人的高低音配合，如何能演奏出和谐的乐章？"

"要是一个男人想要一个或者三个妻子，那该如何？"我问道。

"绝不可能。"他回答道，"就像三加一不可能等于五，人的眼睛不可能看见直线那样。"还没等我打断他的话，他又接着说道，"在每个星期中间的那一天，由于受到自然规律的支配，我们在直线上来回移动的节奏比往日更快，发出的声音也比平时更响。每次这样移动的时间和你数一百零一个数的时间一样长。当这样的大合唱进行到你数第五十一个数的时候，直线国全体子民都会停下手上的工作，然后每一个人都使尽全力发出他们最美妙、最动人的声音。我们年轻人就是在这关键的时刻找到自己的伴侣的。那时，男低音会突然提高三度，男高音则变成女高音，即使相隔遥远，女人们也能立刻辨别出哪个是她们命中注定的白马王子。然后，他们仨人排除千难万险，组合成家庭。在完婚的当日，他们便可以产下三个婴儿。"

"什么？每次都是生三个孩子？"我问道，"难道其中必有一个妻子生下双胞胎？"

"没错！你这个没有低音的怪物！"国王回答道，"倘若一次不生育一男两女，那我们该如何保持性别平衡呢？难道你连最基本的自然规律都忘了吗？"他被我的问题气得说不出话来，停顿了片刻。但是没过多久，他继续说道：

"当然，你也不要以为我们每一个单身汉都能在全国大合唱里第一次求爱，就能找到配偶。事实上，大多数人要尝试好几次才能成功找到意中人。很少有人第一次就能幸运地找到由上天安排的那个对象，然后立刻投入彼此的怀抱开始他们幸福的生活。大多数人的求偶过程都很长。也许求偶男性的声音和其中一个未婚妻配合默契，但是和另一个又不般配，或者起初和两个妻子都不相配，又或者女低音和女高音配合不协调。遇上这种情况时，老天会在每周一次的大合唱后，让这三位恋人的声音变得更加和谐一致。每一次对声音的训练和调整，都会不知不觉地让不完美的一方变得愈加完美。经过如此这般的反复磨合，最终他们一定能达到和谐状态。终于在全国大合唱的某一天，他们三个恋人突然发现彼此之间已完全曲调一致，于是，这仨人迫不及待地欢呼起来。而老天也会祝福这三个新人，并为三个新生儿感到欣喜。"

Ⅱ　我是如何徒劳无功地解释平面国的本质的

我觉得现在有必要去制止一下这位国王的傲慢与无知，好让他了解一些常识，于是我寻思着给他透露一点真相，也就是我们平面国里的状况。于是我说道："尊敬的国王，您是如何区分自己臣民的形状和所处位置的？在来贵国之前，我就看见您的臣民有些是直线，有些是圆点，直线中还有些长短不一。"

"你说的情况根本不可能存在，"国王打断道，"你肯定是产生了幻觉。因为每个人都知道，从本质上来讲，根本就不可能凭借视觉区分直线和圆点。但是听觉倒是有可能，也正是通过这种方式，别人才能够准确知道我的形状。你看，我是一条直线，而且是直线国里最长的直线，空间超过六英寸——"

"是长度超过六英寸。"我大胆地说道。

"愚蠢至极，"他说道，"空间就是长度。下面由你来说，我说完了。"

于是我赶紧道歉，而后他很快就不屑地继续说道："既然你根本听不进我的话，那我就让你用耳朵听一听我两位妻子是如何凭借我的两个声音来确定我的形状的。她们此刻正在六千英里七十码两英尺八英寸之外，一个人在北边，另一个在南边。你听着，我这就召唤她们。"

他窃窃私语了两声，然后就自鸣得意地继续说道："我两个妻子现在就接连听到了我的两个声音，她们会感觉到两个声音之间有时间差。由于在这段时间差里，声音可以传播6457英寸，因此，她们就能推断出我的一个嘴巴离另一个有6457英寸远，这也就是说我的形状有

6457英寸长。显然，我的妻子并不需要每次听到我的声音时都这样计算。她们只需在我们结婚之前算一次就够了。但是，她们可以随时计算。通过这种方法，我可以估计出我每一个男性子民的形状。"

"但是，"我说道，"要是男人用自己的一个声音冒充女人的嗓音，或者他们将自己南边嘴巴发出的声音伪装成北边嘴巴发出声音的回声，那该怎么办呢？这种欺骗行为会不会引起很大的麻烦？难道你们就没有命令所有相邻的两个人用触觉以揭穿这种骗术？"显然，这是一个很愚蠢的问题，因为他们肯定没有用触觉的方法。但是我就是想激怒这位国王。结果，他真的上当了。

"什么？"他惊恐地大喊道，"此话何意？"

"触觉就是触摸，就是身体接触。"我回答道。

"倘若你说的是触摸，"国王说道，"那就让我告诉你这个外地佬，身体接触在我们国家是会被判处死刑的重罪。原因很简单，我们国家必须保护脆弱的妇女，因为她们很容易因身体接触而受伤。也正是由于很难凭借视觉区分男女，我国法律规定男女一律不允许靠得太近，以免破坏两性之间应有的距离。"

"既然我们仅凭听觉就能简单而又准确地算出他人的形状，那么非法的、非自然的亲密接触，即你所说的触摸，还有什么必要呢？至于你所说的由欺骗行为造成的危险，它根本就不存在。因为嗓音是我们每一个人的本性，它不可能被随意改变。好吧，就算我有穿透术，可以通过连续穿透一百万个物体来计算他们的大小和距离。那我得浪费多少时间和精力在这种既笨拙又不精确的方法上！事实上，只要我用耳朵一听，就能给直线国进行人口普查。因为我可以听出每个人肉体上以及精神和心灵上的所有问题。我们的方法就是听，只需用耳朵听！"

说完他就开始倾听起来，仿佛陷入了沉思之中。此时，我只听见一阵微弱的嗡嗡声，仿佛有无数的微型蚂蚱正向我们飞来。

"诚然，"我回答道，"你们的听觉异常灵敏，而且也能弥补你们的很多缺陷。但是请允许我冒昧地指出，你们直线国的生活肯定无比枯燥。除了圆点，你们什么都看不见，甚至连直线都看不见！更不用提何谓直线了！你们也没有我们平面国里那么开阔的视野！与其如此，不如瞎了更好！我承认自己没有你们那种听音辨物的超强听觉，但是你们直线国自认为是听觉盛宴的大合唱，在我听来不过是一团毫无意义的叽叽喳喳声。在我刚进入你的王国时，我就看见你左右摇摆着跳舞，紧邻你左边的是七个男子和一个女子，右边是八个男子和两女子。难道我说的不对吗？"

"没错，"国王答道，"你说的数字和性别都没有错，但是我不明白你说的'左边'和'右边'为何意。我不相信你看得见物体。你怎么可能看见直线呢？那可是一个人的内心啊。你只不过是听见了而已，然后就幻想自己看见了。你说的'左边'和'右边'究竟是何意？朕以为这不过是你们所说的北边和南边罢了。"

"并非如此，"我回答道，"除了你说的北边和南边，我们的确会说左边和右边。"

国王：那就请你给我演示一下，什么是从左到右。

我：不，不，我无法做到。除非你能够从你的直线里跳出来。

国王：跳出直线？你是说跳出直线国？跳出空间？

我：嗯，是的。跳出你的直线国，跳出空间。因为你所说的空间并非真实的空间。真正的空间是平面，而你的空间只不过是一条直线而已。

国王：要是你不能用动作演示什么是左右移动，那就请你用语言解释一下。

我：要是你分不清自己的左和右，我恐怕无法用自己的语言向你解释清楚。但是你绝不能无视它的存在。

国王：我完全无法理解。

我：哎呀！我要怎么说呢？当你往前移动的时候，是否曾经想过往其他的方向移动，转动一下你的眼睛，看看是否能向边侧移动？也就是说，除了向你的直线两头移动之外，你就没有过向两边移动的冲动？

国王：从未有过。你在说什么？一个人怎么可能由里朝外移动？或者说他怎么可能由外朝里移动？

我：好吧，既然语言无法解释清楚这件事，那就让我用行动给你演示一番。我现在就慢慢地朝外移出直线国。

我边说，边开始将身体从直线国里挪出来。只要我身体一部分还在直线国里，这位国王就一直在喊："我看得见你，我还看得见你，你根本就没有动。"但是当我将整个身体移出来以后，他惊恐地大叫道："她不见了，她死了。"

"我没有死，"我回答道，"我只是离开了直线国，也就是你说的空间。但是我此刻正在真正的空间里，并且能够看到所有物体的庐山真面目。我还能看到你们整个直线国的情景，以及它的边，也就是你说的内心。我还可以看见你北边和南边的所有男男女女。我现在来给你描绘一下他们的位置顺序、大小以及彼此之间的间距。"

在滔滔不绝地描述完之后，我不无得意地大喊道："现在你该相信了吧？"说着，我再一次返回到直线国里，并且是回到原先的位置。

但是这位国王却回答道："倘若你是个通情达理的男人（尽管你只能发出一个声音，我已几乎可以肯定你是个女的），哪怕只有一点点脑子，也应该讲点道理。起初你试图说服我在直线国之外另有一条直线，在我熟知的行走方式之外还有另一种方法。然后，我请你用语言描述，或者用行动演示出你所说的另外那条直线。但是，你没有用行动展示，而是使用了些障眼法，把自己变来变去。你也没有用语言清楚地解释，而只是说出了我四十来个随从的个头大小。而这些都是我们都城里妇孺皆知的事情。还有什么比你的所作所为更荒唐，更胆大妄为的事情？收起你的鬼把戏，赶紧滚出我的王国。"

我对他的刚愎自用感到无比愤怒，何况他还对我的性别大放厥词。于是我直接反驳道："愚蠢的家伙，你以为自己是最完美的吗？其实，你才是最低等、最低能的人。你自称有视觉，然而看到的东西除了圆点之外，别无他物！你只能炫耀自己所在的那一条直线。但是，我却能看见很多直线，并且知道世界上还有角，有三角形、正方形、五边形、六边形，甚至还有圆形。我为什么要和你浪费口舌？这就足以证明，我比你高级得多。你不过是一条直线而已，我却是直线的总和，在我们国家别人称呼我正方形。尽管我在平面国贵族阶层中地位不算太高，但是我比你却要高级得多。这也是为什么我要来此给你们启发智力的原因所在。"

国王在听到这些话后，立刻向我扑来，嘴里还发出一阵阵咆哮声，仿佛要从我的对角处将我刺穿一般。这时，他身后的随从们也发出震耳欲聋的助威声。他们的声音越来越大，好似等腰三角形大军，或者五边形炮兵队伍在齐声呐喊一般。我早已被这种情形吓得目瞪口呆，腿脚也开始不听使唤，不停地打着哆嗦。怒吼声越来越响，国王很快就逼近我的跟前，眼看着我就要被他们撕碎。就在这千钧一发的时刻，叮的一声，晨钟将我惊醒。我被拉回了平面国里。

Ⅲ 关于一个来自空间国的陌生人

我从噩梦中惊醒，回到了现实中。

时间依然是一九九九年的最后一天。伴随着滴滴答答的雨声，夜幕早早就降临了。妻子和我依偎而坐[1]，一起回首旧年，憧憬着即将到来的新世纪、新千禧年。

我的四个儿子和两个失去双亲的孙子都已各自回到自己的房间。只有妻子陪在我身旁，同我一起辞旧迎新。

此刻，我脑海里浮现的都是我幼孙嘴里经常冒出的词语。他是个天资聪颖、形状完美的六边形，前途一片光明。我和他的大伯们一直都在教授他视觉识人术。有时，我们故意忽快忽慢地原地旋转，然后问他我们呈现出的形状有何不同。他的回答总是让我心满意足，所以我就忍不住教了他一些可运用于几何学中的算术知识。

我取出九个边长为1英寸的小正方形，然后将它们拼成一个边长3英寸的大正方形。我告诉他，尽管我们无法看见这个正方形的内部大小，但是，我们可以通过将每条边的英寸数平方，计算出它的平方英寸数。我说："因此，我们就可以知道3的平方，即9，代表的就是边长为3英寸的正方形的平方英寸数。"

这个六边形小家伙沉默了片刻，然后问道："但是你已经教过我三次方了，我一直觉得3^3是代表几何学里的某个东西，这个东西到底

---

[1] 我所说的"坐"与你们空间国里的坐下并非同义，因为我们没有腿，既没有坐姿也无法站立。然而，我们"躺着"、"坐着"或者"站着"时，我们身体的明暗度在旁人看来是有区别的。囿于篇幅，我不再赘述细节。

是什么呢？"

　　"什么都不是。"我回答道，"至少在几何学里是如此，因为几何学里只有二维。"接着，我开始给他演示，一个圆点如何通过移动3英寸而变成一条3英寸的线段。该线段可以记作3，然后这条3英寸的线段，又如何通过平移3英寸，而变成一个边长3英寸的正方形。该正方形可以记作3^2。

　　听完后，我的孙子忽然想起了前面的疑问，于是他猛然大声问道："要是一个圆点移动3英寸就可以变成3英寸长的线段，我们用3表示；而3英寸长的线段平移3英寸后又变成边长为3英寸的正方形，我们用3^2表示。同理，3英寸的正方形通过平移（但是我不知道该怎么移）就一定能得到一个每边都是3英寸的某种物体，它可以用3^3来表示。"

　　"快睡觉去，"我对他的话有点气恼，厉声说道，"与其胡言乱语，不如多记数学公理。"

　　于是，我不耐烦地支开了孙子，只留下妻子陪在我身旁。蓦然回首那即将过去的一九九九年，我满怀忐忑地期盼着二〇〇〇年。但是我那机灵的六边形孙子的话却一直回荡在我的耳畔，怎么也挥之不去。直到看见计时半小时的沙漏里的沙子已所剩无几，我才猛然缓过神来。于是我在这个即将过去的世纪里最后一次把沙漏朝北调整了一下方向。我一边挪动沙漏，一边喃喃自语道："这孩子真笨。"

　　就在此时，我突然感觉到房间里出现了一个东西，它让我不禁打了一个寒战。"他才不呢，"妻子大声嚷道，"你如此贬低自己的孙子，简直是有悖人之常情。"但是我没有理会她，而是开始环顾四周，却什么也没看见。然而我感觉那个东西就在我身旁，令人不寒而栗，于是我变得警觉起来。"怎么了？"妻子问道，"又没有风，你在找什么？屋里什么都没有。"

　　我的确什么都没看见，于是只得坐下，继续唠叨道："我是说，这孩子真笨。3^3在几何学中没有任何意义。"话音未落，我就听见一个响亮的声音回答道："这孩子不笨，3^3显然具有几何意义。"

　　妻子和我都听到了这个声音，尽管她听得不甚明白，但是也和我一样看着声音的方向，猛地蹦了起来。这时，我们惊恐地发现眼前居然站着一个图形！起初，从侧面看去，我以为是个妇女。然而，待我定睛一看，才发现他的两端异常暗淡，于是肯定他并非女性。直到看见他明暗渐变的方式与我见过的任何圆形或者规则图形都有所不同时，我才意识到他不是一个普通的圆形。

　　我的妻子却没有我见多识广，也没有足够的耐心注意到对方的不同寻常之处。于是，由于女性天生的妒忌和轻率，她立马断定是一个妇女从某个缝隙里钻进了我们家。"亲爱的，她是怎么进来的？"妻子大喊道，"你不是答应过我，我们的新房子不装通风机的吗？"

　　"我没有装啊，"我说道，"你为什么认为他是个女的？凭我的视觉识人术，我可不这么认为。"

　　"哈哈，我实在是无法容忍你的视觉识人术，"她回答道，"触觉为实，触觉识别一条直线的成功率远胜过视觉识别一个圆形。"这是我们平面国妇女经常挂在嘴边的两个俗语。

　　由于害怕惹恼她，我只好说道："那好，如果真如你所言，那你去和她打声招呼吧。"只见，妻子异常和蔼可亲地走向那个陌生人，说道："女士，请允许我触摸[1]……"突然，她话锋一转，"啊！您不是女士，您也没有角，一个角都没有。难道您是一位纯正的圆形？"

　　"您说的没错，我是圆形，"对方回答道，"而且是平面国里最

[1] 即介绍。——译者注

圆的圆形。准确地讲，我是万圆之圆。"接着，他又用温和的语气说道，"亲爱的女士，我有几句话要带给您的丈夫。不知您能否允许我们单独聊一会儿……"

但是我的妻子却听不进这位令人敬畏的访客委婉的请求，而是一边说自己的独处时间早已结束，另一边还不停地为自己的冒失道歉。但是最终，她还是回到了自己的房间。

这时，我瞥了一眼屋里的沙漏。最后那一点沙子早已落下。第二个新世纪来临了。

IV 陌生人是如何徒劳地向我描述神秘的空间国的

　　未等妻子的脚步声完全消失，我就迫不及待趋步上前，靠近这位陌生人，因为我想近距离地观察他的容貌，并邀请他就坐。他的外貌让我大吃一惊。虽然，他没有任何内角，但是他身体随时产生的明暗渐变却是我见过的任何图形都无法企及的。忽然，我脑海里闪过一个念头：他会不会是一个盗贼或者刺客，又或者是一个冒充圆形声音的不规则等腰三角形，骗过我的门卫进入了我家，现在正要用他锋利的锐角来刺杀我！

　　由于客厅里没有雾（碰巧此时已是十分干燥的季节），我很难凭借视觉识人术来确定他的身份，何况此刻我还离他如此之近。情急之下，我冲到他跟前，冒冒失失地说道："先生，请允许我……"不等自己说完，我就开始触摸起他来。我妻子说的没错——他身上没有任何内角，也没有任何不规则和瑕疵。我从未见过如此完美的圆形。我围着他转了一圈，从他的眼睛开始，直到转回原位。而他只是静静地站着，一动不动。毫无疑问，他是一个完美无瑕的圆形。接下来，我们进行了一段对话。我尽自己所有的记忆，将它原原本本地记录在此，中间只是省去了我一些啰唆的道歉，因为作为一个正方形，我当时为自己贸然触摸他的行为而满怀羞愧。对话是由这位陌生人开始的，他似乎对我拖泥带水的开场白颇为反感。

　　陌生人：你还没将我触摸够吗？你还没有自我介绍吧？
　　我：尊敬的阁下，请原谅我的失礼。我并非不懂上层社会的礼节。只是在下对您的意外来访，实在过于惊讶和紧张。我恳求您不要向任何人说起我的冒失，尤其是我的妻子。在阁下继续问话之前，能否请您屈尊满足在下的好奇心，告诉我您究竟来自何方？

陌生人：来自空间，我来自空间。除此之外，还能是哪里，先生？

我：大人，请原谅我，难道这不就是空间吗，您和在下，此刻不就是身处空间里吗？

陌生人：呸！你对空间了解多少？你解释一下。

我：大人，空间就是高度和宽度的无限延展。

陌生人：瞧，你对空间一无所知。你以为空间只是二维的，但是我今天就要告诉你，它是三维的，它包括长度、宽度以及高度。

我：大人真会开玩笑。我们也会说长度或者高度，宽度或者厚度，这四个词语就是代表二维的啊。

陌生人：我说的不只是三个词语，而是三个维度。

我：请大人解释一下那第三个维度在哪里，我为何不知道它的存在？

陌生人：我就是来自第三维度，它在上方和下方。

我：大人好像是在说北方和南方吧？

陌生人：不对。我指的是你看不见的方向，因为你的侧边没有长眼睛。

我：请原谅我，大人，您只要看我一眼就能发现我的两条边交汇处有一个明显的发光点。

陌生人：是的。但是倘若你想看见空间，就必须要有一只眼睛，一只长在侧面，而不是侧线上的眼睛。这个侧面可能是你们的里面，而在我们空间国里称之为侧面。

我：长在里面的眼睛？我肚子里长眼睛？大人，您不是在开玩笑吧？

陌生人：我可没有心情逗你开心。我说过我来自空间，可惜你无法理解空间的意义。我最近从我们三维国里俯视了你们所谓空间的平面国。我从上方能看到你们说的所有那些立方体（其实不过就是"四边相连"的图形），包括你们的房子、教堂，你们的床头柜和保险箱，甚至是你们的五脏六腑。这些我都看得一清二楚。

我：您只是随口说说的吧？大人。

陌生人：你认为我是信口开河吗？那我这就证明给你看。

当我降落在你们这儿时，我看见了你四个儿子正在各自的房间里，他们都是五边形；你还有两个孙子，都是六边形。我看见你的小孙子先和你们待了一会儿，然后又进入了自己的房间，只留下你和妻子两人。另外，你有三个等腰三角形仆人，他们刚在厨房吃完饭，还有一个小侍从在洗碗。然后，我就来到了你家，你觉得我是怎么来的呢？

我：我想是从屋顶上。

陌生人：错了。你明知自己的屋顶最近刚修葺过，不可能有任何缝隙，就连一个女人都不可能进得来。我说过我是从空间而来。难道我刚才说的关于你小孩和家庭情况的话都不足以让你相信吗？

我：大人肯定知道，住在附近的那些消息灵通人士可以毫不费力就能打听到在下的家庭状况。

陌生人：我如何才能让你相信呢？刚才我只是说了一些基本事实，现在再让我给你演示一番。先生，请听好了。这回你肯定会相信我的。

你们生活在平面之内。你们平面国就是一个巨大的平面，你和你的同胞们都在上面（或者说里面）移动，但是你们既不能从上面，也不能从下方脱离该平面。

　　我不是平面图形，而是立体图形。你称我为圆形，但是事实上我不是圆形，我是由无数个直径逐渐变化的同心圆依次叠加而成的球体，这些圆的直径长度范围在0-13英寸之间。当我切入你们平面国时，正如我现在所做的那样，你能看到的的确只是一个圆形。对于球体而言（这是我在我们国家里的专有名称），倘若他要向平面国的居民证明自己，他只能证明自己是一个圆形。

　　由于我可以看见一切物体，所以能看到你昨晚在梦中游历了直线国，难道你忘了吗？当你进入直线国的时候，你不得不向那位国王证明自己是一条直线，而不是试图证明自己是正方形。因为直线国里没有足够的维度来展示你的全身形状，只能呈现你的一条线段，或者说一小部分。这点难道你忘了吗？同理，由于你们国家只有两个维度，因而也无法展现我的全身，即三维物体，在这里你只能看到我的一小块，或者说一小部分，也就是你所说的圆形。

　　从你的眼神中我看出你还是半信半疑。那就让我来进一步证明我的说法吧。你每次只能看见我的一个圆形，那是因为你的视线无法脱离平面国。但是，当我往上移动的时候，你至少可以看到我的圆形也会随之变小。你看，我现在就往上移动，你会看见我的圆形在逐渐变小，变成一个圆点，直至最后消失。

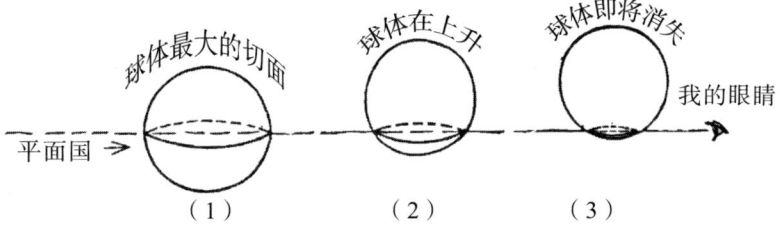

　　我没有看见他"向上移动"的过程，只是看见他的线段在逐渐缩短，直到最后消失不见。于是，我眨了眨眼睛，确信自己不是在做梦。果然不是梦。此时，不知道从哪里（似乎是从我的肚子里）传来一个空灵的声音说道："我是不是消失不见了？现在你相信我了吧？好的，我马上慢慢回到平面国，你就能看到我的圆形会逐渐变大。"

空间国的每一个读者都能轻易地判断出这位神秘来客刚才所讲的既简单又准确。然而，尽管我十分精通平面国的数学，却依然无法理解这简单的事实。上面的示意图可以让任何空间国的小孩明白，面对平面国的居民，球体只有借助图中的三个位置才能解释清楚自己从一个圆形逐渐变为一个圆点的现象。但是，尽管面对事实，我依然无法理解背后的道理所在。我只能认为这个圆形是先将自己变小，然后消失，现在他又重现，并且又将自己慢慢变大。

当他的身形恢复到原来的长短时，他深深地叹了一口气，显然从我的沉默中，他已明白我依旧无法理解他所说的一切。事实上，我现在更相信他根本不是什么圆形，而是一个聪明绝顶的要把戏的人。就像很多老太太说的那样，有些人就是有魔法或者巫术，可以瞒天过海。

他沉默了好一会儿，然后喃喃自语道："要是这些都不行，那就只有最后一个办法了。那就是推理法。"说完，他又陷入沉思中，然后才有了下面的对话。

　　　球体：数学家先生，告诉我，要是一个圆点向北移动时身后留下一条发光的尾迹，你会怎样称呼这条尾迹？

　　　我：一条线段。

　　　球体：一条线段有几个端点？

　　　我：两个。

　　　球体：现在假设这条南北走向的线段由东向西平行移动，即它的每一个圆点都留下一条尾迹。假设这条线段移动的距离和它本身的长度相等，那么你会如何称呼由此形成的那个图形？只要告诉我他的名称就行。

我：正方形。

球体：正方形有几条边？几个角？

我：四条边和四个角。

球体：现在发挥一下你的想象力，假设平面国的一个正方形朝上方平行移动。

我：什么？往北面？

球体：不，不是北面，是朝上方移出平面国。

要是朝北面移动，那么正方形南边的点就会经过北边的点原来所处的位置。但我所说的不是这种方式。

我说的方式是你身上的每一个点（因为你本人就是一个正方形，正好可以做一个类比），即你自称为内脏的部位，向上移动进入空间，如此一来，你的每一个点都不会经过任何其他点原来所处的位置，并且每一个点身后都会画出一条直线。这个类比非常贴切，你应该能听懂的。

我很想冲向这个外来者，将他赶回空间里去，或者将他攥到平面国之外的任何地方，因为再也不用见到他。但是我还是克制住了心中的怒火，只回答道："那按您所说，我向上移动后画出的图形是属于什么性质呢？我想我们平面国的语言还是能够描述出来的吧？"

球体：哦，那当然。其实很简单，我还是来做个类比。我先插一句，画出的不是图形，而是立方体。让我来解释一下，哦，不是我解释，是让类比解释。

我们先从圆点开始，每个圆点只有1个端点。

圆点可以画出有2个端点的线段。

线段可以画出有4个端点的正方形。

1、2、4显然是呈几何级数增长的三个数字，那后面的数字是几？你可以回答吧？

我：8。

球体：完全正确。正方形画出的是一个你暂且不知道名字，但是我们称之为立方体的物体，它有8个端点。现在你明白了吧？

我：这个家伙有边线吗？有内角吗？有你们所说的"端点"吗？

球体：当然有。但是，他的边不是边线，而是我们说的侧面。你应当称这个家伙为立方体。

我：那我按照您说的方式"向上"移动后画出的那个家伙，也就是您所说的立方体，有几条棱呢？

球体：你是数学家！怎么能问如此简单的问题呢？任何物体的侧边都是他背后的一个维度。因此，点之后没有维度，即点没有边；我们可以说线段有两边（因为线段的两头可以被称为两边）；正方形有四条边。所以就是0、2、4，你告诉我这三个数字是什么递增法？

我：等差增长法。

球体：那么下一个数字应该是几？

我：6。

球体：完全正确。现在你已经回答了自己的问题。你产生的立方体会有六条棱，也就是说，你的六个内脏。听明白了吗，嗯？

"你这个妖怪，"我尖叫道，"不管你是什么巫师、骗子、恶魔，还是什么怪物，反正我已经无法再忍受你的鬼把戏了。现在我要和你拼个你死我活。"说着，我猛地冲了上去，决定要将他撵出平面国。

V 这个球体在徒劳解释之后是如何诉诸行动的

但是我的举动不过是徒劳而已。我使出了足以击碎一个普通圆形的力量，顶着自己最坚硬的右侧锐角猛地刺向这个陌生人。但是他却悠然地避开了，既不是向左，也不是向右，而是缓缓地移出了我的世界，直至完全消失不见。此时，我眼前只剩下一片空白，但是这个闯入者的声音却依然没有停歇。

球体：你为何要拒绝接受真相？鉴于你是一个理性之人，而且是一位颇有建树的数学家，我一直希望你做一个智者，并且能成为三维知识的忠实信徒。每隔一千年，我才有机会来传播这个福音。但是，现在我却不知道该如何让你信服。稍等，我有办法了。既然口头传授毫无作用，我相信行动一定可以彰显真理。请听好了，我的朋友。

我已说过，我可以从空间里透视平面国里所有封闭的物体。例如，我看到了你身边的那个橱柜里面放着几个你称为箱子的家具（正如平面国里所有其他物体，它们都没有顶部和底板）。它们里面都装满了财宝。我还看到橱柜里有两个账簿。我马上降落到那个橱柜里，然后取出一个账簿。你半小时前刚将这个橱柜上了锁，并且这把锁就在你身上。但是我会从空间里进去，所以不会撬动你的锁。现在我已经在橱柜里取了账簿。我拿到了。我拿出来了。

我冲到橱柜前，迫不及待地将它打开，发现有一个账本不见了。此时陌生人已站在房间的另一头，对我大声嘲笑。而这时，我发现那个账本正躺在地板上。于是，我走过去把它捡了起来。千真万确，它正是那个丢失的账本。

我惊恐地喘着气，开始怀疑自己是否出现了幻觉。此时，只听到陌生人说道："现在，你肯定相信我了，你说的立体物体都是平面的；而你说的空间只不过是一个广阔的平面而已。我现在身处空间里，可以俯瞰所有物体的内部一切，而你只能看见他们的外表。你可以离开这个平面，只要你下定决心，稍微往上，或者朝下移动一点点即可看见我所见的一切。"

"我站得越高，或者离你们平面国越远，看到的东西就越多，尽管它们会显得更小。我正在上升，我能看见你的六边形邻居，他的家人各处不同的房间。我又看见了剧院里敞开了十扇大门，观众们正鱼贯而出。在另一头，一个圆形正在书房的书堆里埋头苦读。好了，我该回来了。我再给你一个确凿的证据，我要轻轻碰一下你的肚子。你觉得如何？我不会让你受伤，但是你会感到一点疼痛。为了获得心灵启发，这一点点痛也是值得的。"

我还未来得及拒绝，就只觉自己肚子一整剧痛，同时从里面发出一阵魔鬼般的笑声。不一会儿，剧痛又逐渐自然缓解，只感觉一丝闷痛。这时，陌生人又重现我眼前，只见他的身形越变越长，嘴里还说道："我没有弄痛你吧？要是你现在还不相信我，那我真不知道该如何说服你了。你说是吧？"

此时，我早已打定主意。我怎么能受这个骗子摆布，任由他戏弄我的肚子呢？我要用尽全力将他钉到墙上，然后等着救兵来支援！

于是，我再一次挺着自己最坚硬的外角冲向他，同时还大声呼喊着让家人来帮忙。我以为，在我发动攻击之前，他已沉入我们平面之下，因而很难再往上升起。但是他却一直纹丝不动，这时，我似乎听到有人过来帮我，于是我一边加倍用力冲刺过去，一边继续大声呼叫。

我感觉陌生人开始战栗起来，嘴里还仿佛说着："看来，为了让他恢复理智，我只有使出最后一招了。"话音未落，他厉声对我呵斥道："听着，任何其他人都不得知晓我告诉你的一切。马上把你妻子叫开，别让她进来。我绝不会轻易放弃传播三维知识的福音！这一千年才等来的机会，我绝不会轻易浪费！让她走开，要么你就跟我走，去一个你不知道的——三维之国！"

"傻瓜！疯子！异类！"我咆哮道，"我绝不会放过你，我要让你为自己的欺骗行为付出代价！"

"哈哈！真的吗？"陌生人吼道，"还是我来让你见识一下世面吧！滚出你的平面国。一，二，三！成功了！"

VI 我如何来到空间国，又看见了什么

我感到一种无以名状的恐惧。起初我眼前是一片漆黑，接着又出现了一些东西，若隐若现。我看见了一条直线，但感觉又不像是直线。此刻，空间已不再像是我习以为常的那个空间，就连我自己也不再像是自己。当我意识到自己还能说话时，我大声嘶吼起来："这里是阴曹还是地府？"只听见陌生人平静地回答道："都不是，这是知识的王国，是三维之国。睁开你的眼睛，好好看一看。"

我睁开眼睛，仔细一看，果然是一个全新的世界！此时，我眼前正站着一个我曾经推算出并梦想过的完美无瑕的圆形。他的内心，我一览无余，但是，我看不见他的心脏，也看不到他的肺部和血管，只看见一个无比完美的东西，他的美，我简直无法用言语形容。但是，来自空间国的读者们一定知道我所见的只不过是球体的表面。

我对这个向导已心悦诚服，于是我大声喊道："完美无瑕、智慧无穷的神啊！为什么我看得见你的内心，却看不到你的心肺，也看不到你的血管和肝脏？"

他回答道："你以为自己看到了什么，其实你什么都没看见。任何人，包括你，都无法看见我的五脏六腑。我和你们平面国的人完全不在同一等级。我早已告诉过你，我是众圆之首，万圆之圆，在我们国家被称为球体。正如正方体的外表是正方形，球体的外表看起来就像圆形。"

尽管我对这位大师谜语般的话感到疑惑不解，但是我不仅没有生气，反而开始默默地崇拜他。他用更加温和的语气说道："假如你不

能立即明白空间国的奥妙所在，请不要难过。你会逐渐领悟的。我们先回首看看你的出生地——平面国。我会让你看到你时常揣摩但从未曾亲眼见过的内角。"

"绝不可能！"我大声叫道。

但是球体只顾前面带路，而我就像一个梦游的人一样紧随着他，直到他再次开口说道："看，那边就是你的五边形房屋和家人。"

我朝下望去，生平第一次用自己的眼睛看见了自己家人的全貌，而以前我只能猜测他们的长相。此刻，我发现相比眼前的所见，自己以前的推测是多么的盲目和浅陋！我四个儿子正在西北角的卧室里酣睡，而我那两个失去双亲的孙子则睡在南边两个卧室里。我的仆人、管家以及女儿都在各自的房间里。由于我亲爱的妻子听到了我离开时的呼喊声，此刻只有她正在客厅里焦急地来回踱步，祈盼着我的归来。由于我的书童也听到了我的喊声，因而也假惺惺地走过来探视我是否是晕倒了，然而此时他却正在窥视我书房里的橱柜。所有的一切，我都看得真真切切，而不是像以往一样靠推测。当我们进一步靠近时，我甚至可以将橱柜里的物品看得一清二楚，包括里面的两箱金子，以及球体前面提到过的两个账本。

妻子对我的关切让我感动不已，以致我想立刻回去安慰她，但是我却发现自己根本无法移动。"无须担忧你的妻子，"我的向导说道，"她不会等待很久的，现在，我们来俯瞰整个平面国。"

我感觉自己又继续往上升。正如球体所说，我们离观察的物体越远，视野反而变得更加开阔。我出生的整个城市，包括每一栋房屋的内饰和每一个人，都像一个个微型模具让我一览无余。随后，我们继续升向高空，大地的所有奇妙之处，包括她深埋地下的矿藏和大山里的洞穴，都尽收我们眼底。

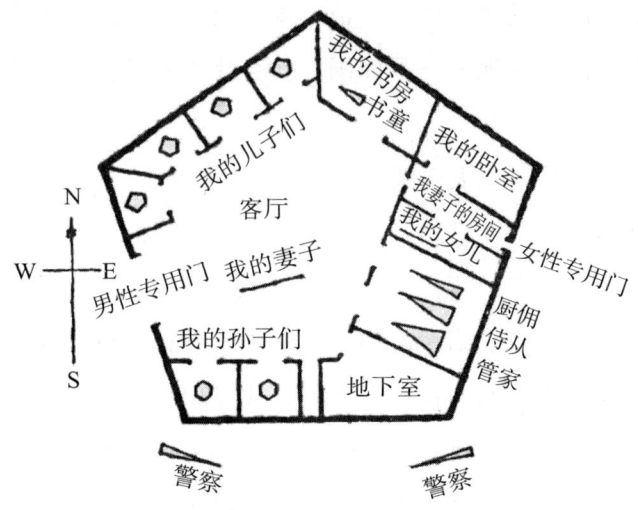

　　面对神奇的大自然，我不禁肃然起敬。于是我对身旁的球体说道："您瞧，我这个凡夫俗子都快成为神仙了。我们国家里的聪明人都说洞察万物（他们称之为全知），是只有上帝才拥有的能力。"球体用略带嘲讽的语气回答道："果真如此？这么说来，我们国家那些扒手和杀人犯都可以被你们国家的聪明人奉若神明了。因为，他们当中，没有哪一个不能看到你所见的一切。相信我，那些聪明人肯定说错了。"

　　我：难道洞察万物是神明以外的人才具有的本领？

　　球体：我不知道。但是，倘若我们国家的一个扒手或者一个杀人犯都能洞见你们国家的一切事物，那么他们绝不应该被奉为神明。你说的全知，在我们空间国里不是一个常用的词语。难道这个词会让你们听起来更富有正义感，更加富有慈悲和爱心，而不至于显得自私吗？显然不会。那什么才可以让你们显得更加神圣呢？

　　我：您说"更加富有慈悲和爱心！"可是，这些都是女性才有的情感！我们都知道圆形是比直线更高等的阶层，因为知识和智慧比情感更受人尊重。

　　球体：虽然我一般不以成就论能力，但是我们空间国里很多最优秀的和最聪明的人都更看重情感，而不是领悟力；更尊重你们所鄙视的直线，而不是备受你们推崇的圆形。不说了，你看那边。你知道那些建筑是什么吗？

　　我放眼望去，看见远处有许多多边形建筑，我认出正中央的那一栋正是平面国的全国大会堂，它被一排排稠密的五边形建筑紧紧包围着。建筑外的街道整齐划一。我知道那肯定是我们的首都。

　　"我们在这儿降落。"向导说道。此刻正是两千年首日的首个时辰。像往常一样，圆形最高领袖们严格遵循传统，正在举行庄严肃穆的秘密会议，正如一千年首日的首个时辰那样，也正如零年首日的首个时辰那样。

　　此时，有一个人正在宣读会议记录。我立刻认出此人正是我的兄弟——一个标准的正方形，他正担任最高委员会的第一书记。他所宣读的内容有史以来从未有任何变动。现在我将它记录在此："国家时常受到各种别有用心之人的威胁，他们谎称自己受到了来自其他世界的启示，然后通过各种活动公然鼓吹谬论、教唆他人。鉴于此，最高委员会在每个千禧年的首日一致决定，向我国每个地区的行政长官传达以下命令：全力搜捕这些误入歧途之人。无须经过任何形式的身体检查，即可采取以下措施：凡是等腰三角形者一律处决；凡是等边三角形者一律鞭笞后收监；凡是正方形或者五边形者一律遣送至当地收容所；凡属更高阶级的违反者，一律直接送至首府，由最高委员会亲自审判。"

　　"你听到自己的下场了吗？死刑或者监禁正在等待你这位三维知

识的忠实传播者。"球体对我说道。此时委员会正在表决通过这一决议。"不见得，"我回答道，"事情已经异常明了，空间国的本质也十分容易理解。我甚至可以让一个小孩都能明白这一切。请允许我现在下去给他们启蒙。"

"现在还不是时候，"我的向导说道，"以后会有机会的。现在我必须要去完成我的使命。你留在这里。"话音未落，他就已经轻盈地跃入了平面国的汪洋之中（请原谅我使用汪洋一词），正好跳入那些委员们的正中央。"我来到此地，"他喊道，"是要向你们宣告三维之国的存在。"

当看到球体的切线不断变长，很多年轻的委员们不禁惊恐地往后躲闪起来。但是随着圆形首脑（他没有丝毫惊慌）的一个手势，只见六个低等的等腰三角形从六个方向直奔球体而去。"我们抓到他了，"他们大声喊道，"不对，是的，我们抓到他了！他要溜了！他不见了！"

"各位议员，"圆形首脑对着中层圆形委员们说道，"无须大惊小怪。只有我一人看过的那份绝密文件告诉我，在前两次千禧年大会上就发生过与此类似的事情。当然，你们也绝不可能将这秘密传出这会场之外。"

然后他提高了嗓门，大声向卫兵命令道："逮捕这些警察，堵上他们的嘴巴。你们知道该如何处置他们。"这些可怜的警察们被迫听到了这些国家机密，却要惨遭如此厄运。圆形首脑宣布完他们的命运后，又对委员们说道："各位委员，委员会的各项议程都已顺利完成。预祝你们新年快乐。"在离会之前，他还对那位书记，即我那优秀却不幸的兄弟，语重心长地说道：他很遗憾，依照先例同时也是出于安全考虑，自己必须判处他终身监禁。但是他又满意地补充道，只要我兄弟不泄露这件事情，他的生命一定会得到保障。

VII 尽管球体给我解释了空间国的其他秘密，但是我想知道更多，结果又如何

当看到自己的兄弟即将被押往监狱时，我试图跳进大会厅去，替他求情，或者至少向他道别。但是我发现自己根本无法行动，因为我的行为完全受到了向导的控制。此刻，他用沮丧的语气说道："不要担心你的兄弟，或许以后你会有充裕的时间去悼念他。随我来。"

于是，我们继续往空中升起。"到目前为止，"球体说道，"我已经将平面图形的里里外外都给你看过了。现在我要给你介绍立方体，让你知道它们是如何构建的。你看，这儿有一些可移动的正方形卡片。我把它们依次垒起来，不是按你说的，往北边排列，而是往上叠加。一张，两张，三张。你看，这就是用正方形累积起来的正方体。它的高度和正方形的长和宽相等。我们称它为立方体。"

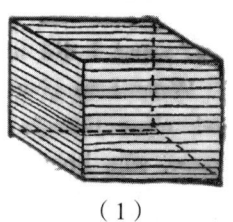

（1）

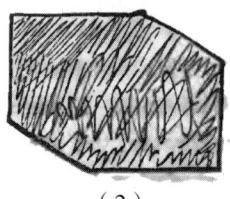

（2）

　　"请原谅我，大人，"我回答道，"但是我的眼睛看见的只是一个不规则图形，它的内部结构展露无遗。我的意思是，我看不见立方体，只是一个如同平面国里的平面图形。它的形状非常不规则，很像是一个恶贯满盈的坏蛋。一看到它，我就觉得恶心。"

　　"没错，"球体说道，"你看它像一个平面图形，那是因为你不习惯光线、阴影以及透视。正如在平面国里的六边形对于不会视觉识人术的人而言，就是一条直线那样。但事实上，这是一个立方体，你可以通过触觉去识别它。"

　　然后，他将我介绍给了这个立方体。我发现这位外形奇特的人果真不是平面图形，而是立体图形。它生有六条棱和由立体角围成的八个顶点。这时，我想起球体说过立方体是由正方形往上平行移动而产生的，于是我不禁为有这样一个出色的后代而倍感自豪。

　　但是我还是无法理解这位大师说的"光线"、"阴影"以及"透视"。所以，我毫不犹豫地说出了自己的疑惑。

　　倘若我将球体给我的解释记录在此，无论我叙述得多么简明扼要，也会让空间国的读者们感到枯燥乏味，因为你们对这三个概念早已耳熟能详。他只是简要地说了几句，然后移动了一些物体以及光线的位置，又让我触摸了它们甚至是他自己的外形，我就完全明白了其中的奥妙。所以我现在可以轻而易举地将圆形和球体，以及平面图形和立体图形区分开来。

　　此时正是我梦想已久的人生重大时刻！面对知识，我绝不会停止探索，因为没有什么比激发一个人的求知欲望后，却不让他进一步探求新知更令人痛苦的事情！我已完全忘记自己的卑微，一心只想成为第二个普罗米修斯，要去唤起平面国和空间国人们的反抗精神，揭穿那个世界只有二维或者三维的弥天大谎。我要至死不渝，坚定执着地寻求历史的真相，即使付出生命的代价也在所不惜。这一信念早已深深地刻在我的脑海中，从未曾有过半点动摇。现在就让我的读者们去评判这一切吧。

球体本来还想继续给我灌输一些关于立方体、圆柱体、圆锥体、金字塔、五面体、六边体、十二面体以及球体构造的知识。但是，我毅然地打断了他。并不是因为我厌倦了这些知识，恰恰相反，而是我对那些他没有讲到的知识更加渴望和向往。

"对不起，"我说道，"我不能再称呼您为完美之神，您能否允许在下看一眼您的内部结构？"

　　球体："我的什么？"

　　我："您的内部结构，即您的胃和内脏。"

　　球体："你是如何想出这些粗俗不堪的问题的？你说我不再是完美之神，又是何意？"

　　我：大人，您用智慧教会我去追求成为一个优秀的、更美丽的、比您都更接近完美的人。您比我们平面国里的所有图形都要高级，您是万圆之圆。但是我相信在您之上肯定也存在一个万球之球，他比空间国里所有的立方体都要高级。尽管我们此刻身处空间内，正在俯视平面国的万物，但是我肯定还有一个比我们现在更高级、更纯洁的地方。尽管我在世界的任何地方，永远都尊称您为哲学家、良师益友，但是您肯定也不打算带我去那个更加广阔的空间，那个多维的天堂。我知道从那里我们可以轻易地俯瞰立体物体的内部一切。甚至是您以及您同辈的五脏六腑，都将被我，一个来自平面国的流放者一览无遗。

　　球体：胡说八道！你这混账！留给你的时间已不多，你却还远远无法胜任给平面国你那些愚昧无知的同胞传播三维福音的重任！

　　我：亲爱的导师，请您不要拒绝我。我知道您有这个能力。

恳请您让我看一眼您的内部结构，我将永远感激涕零，永远做您最温顺的学生和最忠诚的奴隶，并将接受您的一切教诲，将它们一字不漏地传授于他人。

球体：好的，为了让你闭嘴，我现在就可以告诉你，我无法满足你的乞求。难道你要我将自己的五脏六腑掏出来给你看不成？

我：但是老师您已将我带入三维之国，并让我目睹了二维之国里所有同胞的内部结构。为何您不能继续将您的学生带入四维之国，然后一起俯瞰这三维之国，一起领略空间国里那些三维房屋，神奇的大地以及丰富的矿藏。甚至看清每一个立体生命，包括令人敬仰的球体的内部结构。

球体：但是那四维之国在何处呢？

我：我无从知晓，但是您肯定知道。

球体：我也不知道。根本没有这样的地方。你的想法完全是异想天开。

我：您的这番话启发我进一步思考您的教诲。请您不要嘲讽我。我渴望获得更多新知识。毫无疑问，我们无法看见那更高级的空间国，那是因为我们肚子里没有长眼睛。但是，平面国存在的事实，并不能因为直线国那可怜的国君无法左右移动发现它，而被否定。同样，三维之国的存在，也不能因为我无法触摸到它、看见它，而被否定。因此，我肯定有那四维之国的存在，而且您可以通过自己的智慧之眼感知到它。这正是您传授给我的新知。难道您忘记了吗？

在一维世界里，移动的圆点是不是可以产生两个端点？

在二维世界里，移动的直线是不是可以产生四个端点？

在三维世界里，移动的正方形是不是可以产生拥有八个端点的立方体？我不是还目睹了那个神奇的立方体吗？

那么，在四维世界里，一个移动的立方体（啊，为了追求真理，我只好直呼其名，否则我应当说神圣的正方体）是不是可以产生十六个端点？

请您注意这一数列：2、4、8、16。难道这不是几何数列吗？如果不这样称呼，那我应当引述您的原话："严格依此类推。"

此外，您不是教导我说每一条线段都有两个端点，每一个正方形都有四条侧边，每一个正方体都必有六条棱吗？我们再来看这个数列：2、4、6。这不正是一个等差数列吗？这不就是说，神圣的立方体在四维世界里的下一代一定拥有八条侧边。这不也正是您教导我的"严格依此类推"吗？

啊！大人，我才疏学浅，孤陋寡闻，只会做一点逻辑推理。而今我拜在您的门下，就是期望您能证实或者推翻我的论断。倘若我的推论错了，那我愿意认输，不再臆想四维之国。但是，倘若我是正确的，那就请您接受我的论断。

因此，我斗胆问您，您的同胞难道从未曾见过比自己高级的生命降落在空间国里，在封闭的房间里自由出入，就像您进入我家时，不用打开门窗，可以随意出入那样？倘若您拒绝回答我的问题，那我就一直保持沉默。我只需要您给予我一个答复。

球体（沉默片刻后）：的确有过类似的报道，但是凡事人们都有不同的看法。即使面对同样的事实，人们也会做出不同的解读。然而无论有多少种不同的说法，至今尚未有任何人提出四维世界的理论。因此，我们还是少纠结这个问题，言归正传吧。

我：我肯定它一定存在，也相信自己的论断会被证实。敬爱的老师，您不要生气，请再回答我最后一个问题。那些曾拜访过空间国的高级生命不知来自何方，也不知要去往何处。他们是否也是缩小身体，然后消失在那茫茫太空中？就像我现在祈求您教我的那样。

　　球体（情绪激动地）：要是他们真的造访过，那他们肯定也都已消失了。但是，大多数人都说这些报道都是捏造的，是那些疯狂的幻想家想象出来的。这些话你也许听不懂。

　　我：他们真是这么说的？哦，那千万别信他们。倘若真有四维世界，那这个外太空真是一个思想之国，请您带我去这片乐土，在那儿我可以看见所有立体物体的内部结构，我还可以有幸目睹立方体，"严格依此类推"，朝一个全新的方向移动，从而创造出一个比他自己还完美的生命体。这个生命体会有十六个端点和顶角，并且有八个立方体作为周长。在那里，我们还需要往上移动吗？在那个幸福的四维世界里，我们是否又徘徊在五维世界的门槛边，踯躅不前？抑或，我们会得寸进尺，又去探索六维世界，甚至是七维和八维。

　　我不知道自己说了多久，只记得球体在我身旁咆哮着命令我安静下来，并且威胁我要是继续说下去就要严厉惩罚我。但是他说的一切都是徒劳，因为我此时完全沉醉在一片幻想之中，无法自拔。这也许是我的错，但是也怪球体将这些知识传授于我，让我对真理的追求执迷不悟。可惜，好景不长。还没等我说完话，我的身体就受到了一记沉重的打击，紧接着肚子里也开始翻江倒海。我被撞得飞了起来，由于飞行速度太快，以致嘴巴无法发出任何声音。不一会儿，我又感到自己在急速地坠落，我明白回到平面国将是我的宿命。于是，我努力睁开眼睛，最后看了一眼那荒凉而了无生趣的平面国（它马上就要再次成为我的整个世界）。这一幕让我永生难忘。紧接着我只觉眼前一黑，伴随着一声巨大的霹雳声，我失去了知觉。当我苏醒过来时，发现自己又变回了一个只会爬行的普通正方形，正坐在家中的书房里。此时，妻子嘴里正发出欢快的哼哼声，朝我款款走来。

VIII 球体是如何鼓励我追求新世界的

尽管我没有时间多加考虑，但是直觉告诉我，我必须向妻子隐瞒自己的这段经历。并不是我担心她会泄露秘密，而是我断定对于任何平面国的妇女而言，我的奇幻之旅是她们完全无法理解的。于是，我编造了一个故事安慰她。只说我在地窖里不小心掉入了一个暗洞，过了好久才得以脱身。

由于我们国家南方的向北引力极其微弱，即便最普通的妇女都不会相信我杜撰的这个故事，更何况我的妻子，她的智商远在普通妇女之上。虽然她看出了我异乎寻常的兴奋，但是她并没有与我争辩，只是反复地念叨着我肯定是生病了，需要好好休息。等到她离开后，我只觉得整个人昏昏欲睡。但是，就在快要闭上眼睛的时候，我又开始回想起那三维世界来，尤其是正方形移动后变成立方体的那个过程。我对整个过程的印象已很模糊，只记得"向上，不是向北"这个口诀。我相信它就是整个事情的秘诀所在，所以我牢牢地记住了它。于是我嘴里不停地念着"向上，不是向北"，然后就迷迷糊糊地睡着了。

我又做了一个梦。我梦见自己又回到了球体的身旁，他那光彩照人的样子，让我觉得他仿佛已经不再对我生气，而是彻底原谅了我。他指着前方一个异常明亮、但是极其细微的圆点，然后我们一同走了过去。当我们靠近这个圆的时候，我听到他身上正发出如同空间国里大头苍蝇发出的嗡嗡声。这个声音如此微弱，以致在这真空一般的空间里，直到离他只有不超过二十个对角线的距离时，我才听到它。

　　"听着，"我的向导说道，"你虽生在平面国，却见识过直线国，也曾随我登上过空间国。现在，为了让你开开眼界，我要让你了解最低等的世界，也就是小点之国，它是一个没有任何维度的地狱。"

　　"你看那些可怜的小不点。他虽然和我们一样，也有生命，但是却只能躲在这个没有任何维度的角落里。他一个人就组成了一个世界。除了自身之外，他一无所知。他既不知道长度、宽度，也不明白何为高度，因为他从未见识过。他甚至不知道数字2，更不用提复数的概念，因为他自己就代表着一切，也代表着全无。你要留意他的骄傲自满，同时你要学到一个道理，骄傲自大是多么的可怜与无知！有追求比盲目的幸福要好得多。你记住了。"

　　突然，他停了下来。这时我听到从那个微乎其微的小不点发出一阵极其微弱而清晰的叮铃声，如同空间国里的留声机里发出的微弱声音。我仔细一听，原来他在说："生活乐无边，开心每一天。"

　　"这个小家伙说的他是谁？"我问道。

　　"就是他自己，"球体回答道，"难道你从未注意过，婴儿以及那些幼稚的人由于无法将自己和世界区分开来，因而总是用第三人称称呼自己？嘘！"

　　"他就是主宰世界的神，"那个小不点继续自言自语道，"他主宰，他存在；他思考，他说话；他说话，他聆听。他就是思想家、演说家、倾听者。他集思想、语言、听觉于一身，他就是一切。啊！多么幸福啊！他过得多么的幸福啊！"

　　"您为什么不教训一下这个骄傲自满的家伙？"我问道，"告诉他真相，就像您教导我那样。告诉他小点之国的狭隘，让他知道还有更大的世界。"

　　"说得轻巧，"我的恩师说道，"不信你来试一试。"

"安静，安静，你这个可怜的小不点。你自称是万物之神，其实你什么都不是。你所谓的宇宙不过是直线上的一个小点。而直线又不过是一个影子，如果和……"

"嘘，嘘，别浪费口舌了，"球体打断我的话，说道，"听好了，以后要记得和小点之国的国君啰唆讲道理是没有任何作用的。"

当这位国君听到我的话之后，他仿佛更加兴奋，更加骄傲自满了。还未等我说完，他就继续自言自语地说道："啊，思考是多么快乐啊！还有什么是通过思考不能获得的呢？他的思想油然而生，不但表明他出淤泥而不染，而且还让他感到更加幸福！温柔的反抗才会赢得胜利！集所有于一身是多么神圣的创造力啊！存在就是最大的快乐！"

"你看，"恩师说道，"你的话根本没用。他根本无法理解你的话，还以为是自己说的话，因为他除了自身之外任何事物都感知不到。他洋洋得意地以为他的思考就是一种创造力。我们还是让这位小点之国的国君继续沉浸在自己无知的自满之中吧。你我根本无法拯救他。

之后，我们就缓缓地飞回平面国。途中，我的导师一直用他温和的语气教导我，他说他支持我探索新世界，然后去教育他人追求新知识。他承认自己起初对我关于四维世界的论断很不高兴，但是，他认识到这是一个全新的观点，并且愿意向我认错并接受它。接着，他又鼓励我去探寻比我所有见过的世界更高级的未知空间。他给我解释了如何通过移动立方体产生超立方体，然后通过移动超立方体又产生更高级的立方体，他的方法就是"严格依此类推"，其过程简单得连妇女都能毫不费力地理解。

IX 我是如何尝试去教我的孙子三维理论的，又取得了什么成果

我从甜美的梦中醒来，开始思考导师交给我的这个光荣使命。我决心立刻就动手，向整个平面国传播福音，因为我觉得即便是女人和士兵也应该成为三维福音的信徒。于是，我决定先从我的妻子开始。

正当我制定好了自己的行动计划时，突然街上传来了要求人们保持安静的命令声。紧接着我又听到一个更洪亮的说话声，原来是一个传令员在发布公告。待我仔细一听，发现他宣布的正是委员会的决议：任何蛊惑人心，并伪称收到了来自另一个国家的启示的人，一律逮捕、监禁或处决。

我陷入了沉思。看来这个光荣使命并非那么容易完成。为了避开风险，我最好不去提及任何启示，只是继续展开我的阐述。毕竟，这个方法看起来虽然简单，却很有成效，因此，即便我不去公开传播三维启示，对传递福音也没任何损失。"向上，而不是向北"——这就是秘诀所在。在入睡前，我对这个口诀记忆犹新；当我第一次从睡梦中醒来时，那口诀依然像数学公理那样清晰明了；但是不知何故，我如今居然不太敢确信了。此时，我的妻子刚好走进房间来，在我们说了几句家常话之后，我决定还是不从她开始了。

我的五边形儿子们都是为人正直、名声显赫的医生，却不擅长数学，因而不符合我的要求。此时，我突然想到我年幼温顺的六边形孙子，他对数学刚开始感兴趣，将是我最合适的学生。我早熟的小孙子

对3³含义的解释和球体的理解是一致的，为什么不对他进行我的第一次试验呢？他还仅仅是个小男孩，和他讨论这件事情，绝对安全；因为他完全不知道委员会的禁令。但是我却不放心和我的儿子们一起探讨三维知识，因为他们誓死效忠圆形的统治，一旦他们发现我在散布煽动性的异端言论，我很难确保他们不会把我交给地方行政长官。

但是首先我得满足我妻子的好奇心，因为她一直很想知道为何圆形要和我秘谈，以及他又是如何进到我们屋子的。我给她精心编造了一个解释，细节就不展开了，我担心这个解释和空间国读者们期望的真相会不太一致。但我必须自豪地说，我最终还是成功地说服了她继续安安静静地回去做她的家务，不要再打听任何有关三维世界的信息。这之后，我立刻派人召来了我的孙子。说实话，我感觉所有的记忆正奇怪地从我脑中悄悄地溜走，它们已变得像一个让人捉摸不透、却十分诱人的美梦。我迫不及待地要向我的第一个弟子传播福音。

当我孙子走进房间后，我小心翼翼地关好门。然后，我在他旁边坐下，顺手拿起一个数学写字板（你们称它为直线），告诉他我们要继续头天的课程。我再次教他一维里的点运动后如何产生直一条直线，二维里的直线如何产生一个正方形。说完后，我干咳了一声，说道："你这个调皮鬼不是想让我相信正方形也可能会以相同的方式运动，'向上，而不是向北'的方式产生另一个图形，一个超越正方形的图形吗？现在，你把这个猜想再说一遍，你这个小淘气。"

就在这时，我们再次听到街上传令员发出"是的，是的"的赞同声，他还在宣布委员会颁布的禁令。我的孙子尽管年纪尚幼，却异乎寻常的聪明，而且又成长在一个对圆形政府权威无比崇敬的环境中。他似乎敏锐地察觉到了当前的局势，这是我始料未及的。他一直默不作声，直到朗读决议的声音逐渐远去，他才大声哭了起来。"爷爷，"他说，"我昨天只是开个玩笑，当然没有其他的意思，当时我们都完全不知道有这个新法令，而且我也没有说过关于三维的任何事情，我绝对没说过什么'向上，而不是向北'的话，你也知道这句话根本就说不通，一个东西怎么能向上运动而不是向北运动呢？向上，而不是向北！虽然我只是一个小孩子，但也不至于那么懵懂。多傻啊，哈哈哈！"

　　"一点也不傻，"我开始发脾气了，"我拿这个正方形给你举个例子。"说着，我拿起手边一个可移动的正方形。"我要移动它，你看，不是向北而是——对，我向上移动它——也就是说，不是向北，而是向其他方向移动它——不是这样子，而是——"我语无伦次地向他解释，手里还漫无目的地摇晃着那个正方形。我的孙子觉得我太滑稽了，于是忍不住大声笑了起来。他说我不是在教他知识，而是在逗他玩。说着他打开门跑出了房间。我第一次试图把小学生变成三维福音信徒的尝试，就这样结束了。

X 我是如何尝试用其他方法传播
三维理论的，又导致了什么结果

向孙子传播三维福音的失败经历，打消了我向其他家庭成员透露这个秘密的念头，但我也没有因此感到绝望。我只意识到，我不能完全依赖于"向上，而不是向北"这个秘诀。我必须努力去寻求一种可以让公众在整体上对三维理论有清晰认识的演示方法。为此，我似乎很有必要通过撰写文章宣扬我的思想。

所以我暗地里花费数月时间完成了一篇论述三维之谜的文章。为了避免触及法律，我没有提及任何一个物理维度，而是描述了一个理想国。从理论上讲，我们可以从这个国家俯视平面国，同时可以看到所有物体的内部结构。而且在这里，还存在一种被六个正方形包围的图形，这个图形包含八个端点，但是在写这本书的时候，我悲哀地发现自己根本就画不出这样的图形，而这个图形对我的写作目的却十分关键。因为在我们平面国，这里当然没写字板，只有直线；没有图形，只有直线，所有的东西都是一条直线，只能靠尺寸大小和明亮度来区分各种物体。所以，当我写完这篇文章（它的标题为"从平面国到理想国"）时，我知道大多数人将无法理解我的意思。

乌云笼罩着我的生活，让我感觉不到一丝快乐。面对眼前所有的景象，我时刻有一种背叛平面国的冲动，因为我总是情不自禁将自己在二维世界里看到的物体与三维世界里的作比较。就这样，我逐渐疏远了自己的客户，也荒废了事业，完全沉浸在自己的奇幻之旅中，但是，我却不能将它分享给任何其他人。我发现自己日益难以追忆在三维世界里的那些盛景。

有一天，大约是我从空间国返回后的第十一个月，我试图闭上眼睛回忆起一个立方体，但是没有成功。尽管之后我做到了，但我当时（直到现在）却不敢确定那就是三维国里的正方体。于是我倍感忧虑，我决意要让自己有所作为，但是该如何作为，我还不得而知。只要能让世人相信三维世界的存在，哪怕为之牺牲生命，我也在所不惜。但若是我的孙子都无法相信我，我又如何能让国家最高阶层的圆形信服呢？

也许是由于我过于冲动，因而有时候会无意间发表一些危险的言论。虽然我的言行还够不上叛国罪，但显然是离经叛道。我也敏锐地觉察到了自己的危险处境，但我还是无法克制自我，依然时不时讲出一些可疑甚至煽动的话语，即便是在最高级多边形和圆形的面前。比如，当人们讨论如何治疗那些自称可以看见事物内部的疯子时，我就引用一位古代圆形的话——先知和受启蒙的人大多数都被认为是疯子。我有时还会情不自禁地说出"能看透事物本质的眼睛"和"一切都可见的国家"这类的话。甚至，有一两次我居然将禁语"三维和四维"脱口而出。最终，我如愿以偿。事情的原委是，在某个极其愚蠢的人阅读了一篇别有用心的论文（此文不但准确解释了上天把维度限制为二的原因，而且还详细阐明了为何只有上帝才有全知的能力）之后，我们当地的推理社团在地方长官的宅邸中举行了一场聚会。在那次聚会上，我忘乎所以，居然将自己和球体在空间的旅行经历，还有我们如何去全国大会堂，然后回到空间，又返回家中，以及我亲历的和臆想的所见所闻，和盘托出。的确，起初我只是假装在讲述一个虚构人物的历险记，但是我的热情很快就让我脱下了所有伪装。最后，在一段热情洋溢的总结中，我劝导所有的听众应抛弃他们的无知，成为三维福音的信徒。

还用说我的下场吗？我立即就被逮捕押送至委员会面前了？

翌日清晨，我站在几个月前我和球体一起站过的位置上。委员会允许我继续做自我辩护，期间没有人问我问题，也没人打断我。但是从一开始我就预见了我的命运，因为委员会主席注意到在场的一个警卫来自高级警察部队（他的角度很规则，顶角在55°以下）后，命令他在我做自我辩护之前就离开现场，由一个只有2°或3°内角的下等卫兵接替了他的岗位。我当然明白这个举动的含义。毫无疑问，我将面临处决或监禁，而且我的故事将不会被世人所知，因为在场听到我故事的所有官员都会被同时消灭。无怪乎，主席要让地位更卑微的牺牲品给我陪葬。

在我的总结陈词结束之后，主席或许察觉到一些地位较低的圆形委员已被我的慷慨陈词打动。于是，他问了我两个问题：

1. 我能否暗示我说的"向上，而不是向北"是哪个方向？

2. 我能否需要通过示意图或者描述（而不是列举抽象的边或角）来描绘出我所称为立方体的图形？

我义正词严地回答道：我已陈述完毕，并决心为真理献身，我坚信真理的事业必将获胜。

主席说他非常敬仰我的献身精神，认为我已经做到至善至美。他还说我必须被判处永久监禁，但假若真理认为我应该获释，并向世界传播福音，那么他就应当立刻显灵。接着，他还保证不会让我遭受酷刑，因为它对防止越狱毫无意义。而且他还准许我时常与我监中的兄弟相见，除非我自己犯错，否则我会一直享有这一特权。

七年过去了，我依然困在这监狱。除了狱卒之外，我没有任何同伴（除了偶尔和我见面的兄弟）。我哥哥是最优秀的正方形中的一员，他为人正直，深明大义，性格开朗，又讲兄弟情义。但我必须坦白我与哥哥的每周见面，最少在某一方面，带给我的却是极大的痛苦。当初球体在大会堂里证明他自己的时候，我哥哥也在场，他看到了球体不断变化的切面，也听见了球体向圆形解释这一现象发生的缘由。这七年来，我每一周都在向他反复证明我在思想启蒙中肩负的重任，不厌其烦地描述空间国里的盛况，以及通过类比解释立方体存在的证据。但是我很惭愧地承认，我哥哥到现在都没能掌握三维世界的本质，并且他也坦承自己根本不相信球体的存在。

似乎今后我也无法转变任何人的思想。如此说来，千禧年的启示对我来说没有任何意义。

空间国的普罗米修斯为我们盗来了知识的火种，而我作为平面国可怜的普罗米修斯，却因向自己的同胞传播福音而沦为阶下囚。但是我希望这一份回忆录，能以某种未知的方式，启发某个世界里人们的思想，并且唤醒那些被束缚在有限维度里的反抗者的斗志。

那是我梦寐以求的结果。可是，我又不敢抱有太多奢望。有时我深感重任在肩，因为我不敢保证自己能准确回忆起那只有一面之交，却让我心驰神往的立方体形状。在睡梦中，那神秘的口诀"向上，而不是向北"就像一个吞噬灵魂的恶魔时刻缠绕着我。当立方体和球体的形象在我脑海中变得日渐模糊时，当三维世界变得和一维国或零维国一样如同空中楼阁时，我的意志也会变得脆弱。但是，即便禁锢我自由的狱中高墙，以及我此刻写作用的笔记本，连同平面国里那所有的现实，都只不过是一个虚无缥缈的黄粱美梦，我也将义无反顾地去追逐那真理的脚步，死而后已。

FLATLAND

A Romance of Many Dimensions

A SQUARE(*Edwin A.Abbott*)

To

The Inhabitants of SPACE IN GENERAL

And H. C. IN PARTICULAR

This Work is Dedicated

By a Humble Native of Flatland

In the Hope that

Even as he was Initiated into the Mysteries

Of THREE Dimensions

Having been previously conversant

With ONLY Two

So the Citizens of that Celestial Region

May aspire yet higher and higher

To the Secrets of FOUR FIVE OR EVEN Six Dimensions

Thereby contributing

To the Enlargement of THE IMAGINATION

And the possible Development

Of that most rare and excellent Gift of MODESTY

Among the Superior Races

Of Solid Humanity

PART I   THIS WORLD

"Be patient, for the world is broad and wide."

§ 1.—Of the Nature of Flatland.

I CALL our world Flatland, not because we call it so, but to make its nature clearer to you, my happy readers, who are privileged to live in Space.

Imagine a vast sheet of paper on which straight Lines, Triangles, Squares, Pentagons, Hexagons, and other figures, instead of remaining fixed in their places, move freely about, on or in the surface, but without the power of rising above or sinking below it, very much like shadows —only hard and with luminous edges—and you will then have a pretty correct notion of my country and countrymen. Alas, a few years ago, I should have said "my universe": but now my mind has been opened to higher views of things.

In such a country, you will perceive at once that it is impossible that there should be anything of what you call a "solid" kind; but I dare say you will suppose that we could at least distinguish by sight the Triangles Squares and other figures moving about as I have described them. On the contrary, we could see nothing of the kind, not at least so as to distinguish one figure from another. Nothing was visible, nor could be visible, to us, except straight Lines; and the necessity of this I will speedily demonstrate.

Place a penny on the middle of one of your tables in Space; and leaning over it, look down upon it. It will appear a circle.

But now, drawing back to the edge of the table, gradually lower your eye (thus bringing yourself more and more into the condition of the inhabitants of Flatland), and you will find the penny becoming more and more oval to your view; and at last when you have placed your eye exactly on the edge of the table (so that you are, as it were, actually a Flatland citizen) the penny will then have ceased to appear oval at all, and will have become, so far as you can see, a straight line.

The same thing would happen if you were to treat in the same way a Triangle, or Square, or any other figure cut out of pasteboard. As soon as you look at it with your eye on the edge of the table, you will find that it ceases to appear to you a figure, and that it becomes in appearance a straight line. Take for example an equilateral Triangle—who represents with us a Tradesman of the respectable class. Fig. I represents the Tradesman as you would see him while you were bending over him from above; figs. 2 and 3 represent the Tradesman, as you would see him if your eye were close to the level, or all but on the level of the table; and if your eye were quite on the level of the table (and that is how we see him in Flatland) you would see nothing but a straight line.

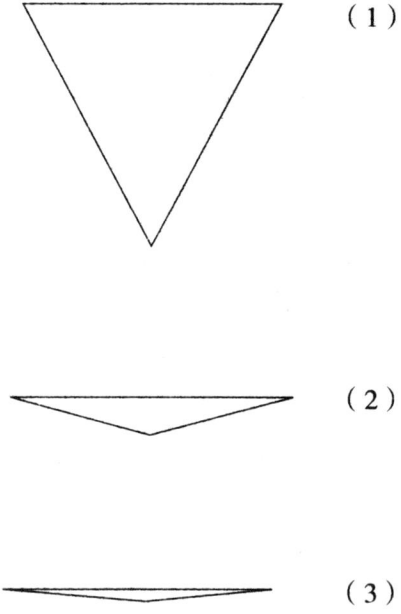

(1)

(2)

(3)

When I was in Spaceland I heard that your sailors have very similar experiences while they traverse your seas and discern some distant island or coast lying on the horizon. The far-off land may have bays, forelands, angles in and out to any number and extent; yet at a distance you see none of these (unless indeed your sun shines bright upon them revealing the projections and retirements by means of light and shade), nothing but a grey unbroken line upon the water.

Well, that is just what we see when one of our triangular or other acquaintances comes towards us in Flatland. As there is neither sun with us, nor any light of such a kind as to make shadows, we have none of the helps to the sight that you have in Spaceland. If our friend comes close to us we see his line becomes larger; if he leaves us it becomes smaller: but still he looks like a straight line; be he a Triangle, Square, Pentagon, Hexagon, Circle, what you will—a straight Line he looks and nothing else.

You may perhaps ask how under these disadvantageous circumstances we are able to distinguish our friends from one another: but the answer to this very natural question will be more fitly and easily given when I come to describe the inhabitants of Flatland. For the present let me defer this subject, and say a word or two about the climate and houses in our country.

§ 2.—Of the climate and houses in Flatland.

As with you, so also with us, there are four points of the compass North, South, East, and West.

There being no sun nor other heavenly bodies, it is impossible for us to determine the North in the usual way; but we have a method of our own. By a Law of Nature with us, there is a constant attraction to the South; and, although in temperate climates this is very slight—so that even a Woman in reasonable health can journey several furlongs northward without much difficulty—yet the hampering effect of the southward attraction is quite sufficient to serve as a compass in most parts of our earth. Moreover the rain (which falls at stated intervals) coming always from the North, is an additional assistance; and in the towns we have the guidance of the houses, which of course have their side-walls running for the most part North and South, so that the roofs may keep off the rain from the North. In the country, where there are no houses, the trunks of the trees serve as some sort of guide. Altogether, we have not so much difficulty as might be expected in determining our bearings.

Yet in our more temperate regions, in which the southward attraction is hardly felt, walking sometimes in a perfectly desolate plain where there have been no houses nor trees to guide me, I have been occasionally compelled to remain stationary for hours together, waiting till the rain came before continuing my journey. On the weak and aged, and especially on delicate Females, the force of attraction tells much more heavily than on the robust of the Male Sex, so that it is a point of breeding, if you meet a Lady in the street, always to give her the North side of the way —by no means an easy thing to do always at short notice when you are in rude health and in a climate where it is difficult to tell your North from your South.

Windows there are none in our houses: for the light comes to us alike in our homes and out of them, by day and by night, equally at all times and in all places, whence we know not. It was in old days, with our learned men, an interesting and oft-investigated question. What is the origin of light; and the solution of it has been repeatedly attempted, with no other result than to crowd our lunatic asylums with the would-be solvers. Hence, after fruitless attempts to suppress such investigations indirectly by making them liable to a heavy tax, the Legislature, in comparatively recent times, absolutely prohibited them. I, alas I alone in Flatland—know now only too well the true solution of this mysterious problem; but my knowledge cannot be made intelligible to a single one of my countrymen; and I am mocked at—I, the sole possessor of the truths of Space and of the theory of the introduction of Light from the world of Three Dimensions—as if I were the maddest of the mad! But a truce to these painful digressions: let me return to our houses.

The most common form for the construction of a house is five-sided or pentagonal, as in the annexed figure. The two Northern sides RO, OF, constitute the roof, and for the most part have no doors; on the East is a small door for the Women; on the West a much larger one for the Men; the South side or floor is usually doorless.

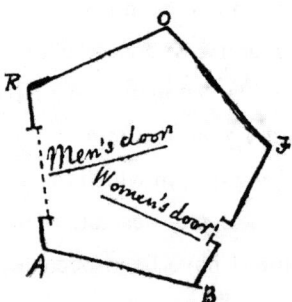

Square and triangular houses are not allowed, and for this reason. The angles of a Square (and still more those of an equilateral Triangle) being much more pointed than those of a Pentagon, and the lines of inanimate objects (such as houses) being dimmer than the lines of Men and Women, it follows that there is no little danger lest the points of a square or triangular house residence might do serious injury to an inconsiderate or perhaps absent-minded traveller suddenly running against them: and therefore, as early as the eleventh century of our era, triangular houses were universally forbidden by Law, the only exceptions being fortifications, powder-magazines, barracks, and other state buildings, which it is not desirable that the general public should approach without circumspection.

At this period, square houses were still everywhere permitted, though discouraged by a special tax. But, about three centuries afterwards, the Law decided that in all towns containing a population above ten thousand, the angle of a Pentagon was the smallest house-angle that could be allowed consistently with the public safety. The good sense of the community has seconded the efforts of the Legislature; and now, even in the country, the pentagonal construction has superseded every other. It is only now and then in some very remote and backward agricultural district that an antiquarian may still discover a square house.

§ 3.—Concerning the Inhabitants of Flatland.

The greatest length or breadth of a full-grown inhabitant of Flatland may be estimated at about eleven of your inches. Twelve inches may be regarded as a maximum.

Our Women are Straight Lines.

Our Soldiers and Lowest Classes of Workmen are Triangles with two equal sides, each about eleven inches long, and a base or third side so short (often not exceeding half an inch) that they form at their vertices a very sharp and formidable angle. Indeed when their bases are of the most degraded type (not more than the eighth part of an inch in size), they can hardly be distinguished from Straight Lines or Women; so extremely pointed are their vertices. With us, as with you, these Triangles are distinguished from others by being called Isosceles; and by this name I shall refer to them in the following pages.

Our Middle Class consists of Equilateral or Equal-sided Triangles.

Our Professional Men and Gentlemen are Squares (to which class I myself belong) and Five-sided figures or Pentagons.

Next above these come the Nobility, of whom there are several degrees, beginning at Six-sided Figures, or Hexagons, and from thence rising in the number of their sides till they receive the honorable title of Polygonal, or many-sided. Finally when the number of the sides becomes so numerous, and the sides themselves so small, that the figure cannot be distinguished from a circle, he is included in the Circular or Priestly order; and this is the highest class of all.

It is a Law of Nature with us that a male child shall have one more side than his father, so that each generation shall rise (as a rule) one step in the scale of development and nobility. Thus the son of a Square is a Pentagon; the son of a Pentagon, a Hexagon; and so on.

But this rule applies not always to the Tradesmen, and still less often to the Soldiers, and to the Workmen; who indeed can hardly be said to deserve the name of human Figures, since they have not all their sides equal. With them therefore the Law of Nature does not hold; and the son of an Isosceles (i.e. a Triangle with two sides equal) remains Isosceles still. Nevertheless, all hope is not shut out, even from the Isosceles, that his posterity may ultimately rise: above his degraded condition. For, after a long series of military successes, or diligent and skilful labour, it is generally found that the more intelligent among the Artisan and Soldier classes manifest a slight increase of their third side or base, and a shrinkage of the two other sides. Intermarriages (arranged by the Priests) between the sons and daughters of these more intellectual members of the lower classes generally result in an offspring approximating still more to the type of the Equal-sided Triangle.

Rarely—in proportion to the vast number of Isosceles births—is a genuine and certifiable Equal-sided Triangle produced from Isosceles parents[1]. Such a birth requires, as its antecedents, not only a series of carefully arranged intermarriages, but also a long-continued exercise of frugality and self-control on the part of the would-be ancestors of the coming Equilateral, and a patient, systematic, and continuous development of the Isosceles intellect through many generations.

The birth of a True Equilateral Triangle from Isosceles parents is the subject of rejoicing in our country for many furlongs round. After a strict examination conducted by the Sanitary and Social Board, the infant, if certified as Regular, is with solemn ceremonial admitted into the class of Equilaterals. He is then immediately taken from his proud yet sorrowing parents and adopted by some childless Equilateral, who is bound by oath never to permit the child henceforth to enter his former home or so much as to look upon his relations again, for fear lest the freshly developed organism may, by force of unconscious imitation, fall back again into his hereditary level.

The occasional emergence of an Isosceles from the ranks of his serf-born

---

[1] "What need of a certificate?" a Spaceland critic may ask: "Is not the procreation of a Square Son a certificate from Nature herself, proving the Equal-sidedness of the Father?" I reply that no Lady of any position will marry an uncertified Triangle. Square offspring has sometimes resulted from a slightly Irregular Triangle: but in almost every such case the Irregularity of the first generation is visited on the third; which either fails to attain the Pentagonal rank, or relapses to the Triangular.

ancestors, is welcomed not only by the poor serfs themselves, as a gleam of
light and hope shed upon the monotonous squalor of their existence, but also by
the Aristocracy at large; for all the higher classes are well aware that these rare
phenomena, while they do little or nothing to vulgarize their own privileges,
serve as a most useful barrier against revolution from below.

Had the acute-angled rabble been all, without exception, absolutely destitute
of hope and of ambition, they might have found leaders in some of their many
seditious outbreaks, so able as to render their superior numbers and strength
too much even for the wisdom of the Circles. But a wise ordinance of Nature
has decreed that, in proportion as the working-classes increase in intelligence,
knowledge, and all virtue, in that same proportion their acute angle (which
makes them physically terrible) shall increase also and approximate to the
harmless angle of the Equilateral Triangle. Thus, in the most brutal and
formidable of the soldier class creatures almost on a level with women in their
lack of intelligence—it is found that, as they wax in the mental ability necessary
to employ their tremendous penetrating power to advantage, so do they wane in
the power of penetration itself.

How admirable is this Law of Compensation! And how perfect a proof of
the natural fitness and, I may almost say, the divine origin of the aristocratic
constitution of the States in Flatland! By a judicious use of this Law of Nature,
the Polygons and Circles are almost always able to stifle sedition in its very
cradle, taking advantage of the irrepressible and boundless hopefulness of the
human mind. Art also comes to the aid of Law and Order. It is generally found
possible—by a little artificial compression or expansion on the part of the
State physicians—to make some of the more intelligent leaders of a rebellion
perfectly Regular, and to admit them at once into the privileged classes; a much
larger number, who are still below the standard, allured by the prospect of being
ultimately ennobled, are induced to enter the State Hospitals, where they are
kept in honorable confinement for life; one or two alone of the more obstinate,
foolish, and hopelessly irregular are led to execution.

Then the wretched rabble of the Isosceles, planless and leaderless, are either
transfixed without resistance by the small body of their brethren whom the Chief
Circle keeps in pay for emergencies of this kind; or else more often, by means

of jealousies and suspicions skillfully fomented among them by the Circular party, they are stirred to mutual warfare, and perish by one another's angles. No less than one hundred and twenty rebellions are recorded in our annals, besides minor outbreaks numbered at two hundred and thirty-five; and they have all ended thus.

§ 4.—Concerning the Women.

If our highly pointed Triangles of the Soldier class are formidable, it may be readily inferred that far more formidable are our Women. For, if a Soldier is a wedge, a Woman is a needle; being, so to speak, *all* point, at least at the two extremities. Add to this the power of making herself practically invisible at will, and you will perceive that a Female, in Flatland, is a creature by no means to be trifled with.

But here, perhaps, some of my younger Readers may ask *how* a woman in Flatland can make herself invisible. This ought, I think, to be apparent without any explanation. However, a few words will make it clear to the most unreflecting.

Place a needle on a table. Then, with your eye on the level of the table, look at it side-ways, and you see the whole length of it; but look at it end-ways, and you see nothing but a point: it has become practically invisible. Just so is it with one of our Women. When her side is turned towards us, we see her as a straight line; when the end containing her eye or mouth—for with us these two organs are identical—is the part that meets our eye, then we see nothing but a highly lustrous point; but when the back is presented to our view, then—being only sub-lustrous, and, indeed, almost as dim as an inanimate object—her hinder extremity serves her as a kind of Invisible Cap.

The dangers to which we are exposed from our Women must now be manifest to the meanest capacity in Spaceland. If even the angle of a respectable Triangle in the middle class is not without its dangers; if to run against a Working Man involves a gash; if collision with an Officer of the military class necessitates a serious wound; if a mere touch from the vertex of a Private Soldier brings with it danger of death; — what can it be to run against a Woman, except absolute and immediate destruction? And when a Woman is invisible, or visible only as a dim sub-lustrous point, how difficult must it be, even for the most cautious, always to avoid collision!

Many are the enactments made at different times in the different States of Flatland, in order to minimize this peril; and in the Southern and less temperate climates, where the force of gravitation is greater, and human beings more liable to casual and involuntary motions, the Laws concerning Women are naturally much more stringent. But a general view of the Code may be obtained from the following summary:—

1. Every house shall have one entrance in the Eastern side, for the use of Females only; by which all females shall enter "in a becoming and respectful manner"[1] and not by the Men's or Western door.

2. No Female shall walk in any public place without continually keeping up her Peace-cry, under penalty of death.

3. Any Female, duly certified to be suffering from St. Vitus's Dance, fits, chronic cold accompanied by violent sneezing, or any disease necessitating involuntary motions, shall be instantly destroyed.

In some of the States there is an additional Law forbidding Females, under penalty of death, from walking or standing in any public place without moving their backs constantly from right to left so as to indicate their presence to those 'behind them; others oblige a Woman, when traveling, to be followed by one of her sons, or servants, or by her husband; others confine Women altogether to their houses except during the religious festivals. But it has been found by the wisest of our Circles or Statesmen that the multiplication of restrictions on Females tends not only to the debilitation and diminution of the race, but also to the increase of domestic murders to such an extent that a State loses more than it gains by a too prohibitive Code.

For whenever the temper of the Women is thus exasperated by confinement at home or hampering regulations abroad, they are apt to vent their spleen upon their husbands and children; and in the less temperate climates the whole male population of a village has been sometimes destroyed in one or two hours of simultaneous female outbreak. Hence the Three Laws, mentioned above, suffice

---

[1] When I was in Spaceland I understood that some of your Priestly Circles have in the same way a separate entrance for Villagers, Fanners, and Teachers of Board Schools (Spectator, Sept. 1884, p. 1255) that they may "approach in a becoming and respectful manner."

for the better regulated States, and may be accepted as a rough exemplification of our Female Code.

After all, our principal safeguard is found, not in Legislature, but in the interests of the Women themselves. For, although they can inflict instantaneous death by a retrograde movement, yet unless they can at once disengage their stinging extremity from the struggling body of their victim, their own frail bodies are liable to be shattered.

The power of Fashion is also on our side. I pointed out that in some less civilised States no female is suffered to stand in any public place without swaying her back from right to left. This practice has been universal among ladies of any pretensions to breeding in all well-governed States, as far back as the memory of Figures can reach. It is considered a disgrace to any State that legislation should have to enforce what ought to be, and is in every respectable female, a natural instinct. The rhythmical and, if I may so say, well-modulated undulation of the back in our ladies of Circular rank is envied and imitated by the wife of a common Equilateral, who can achieve nothing beyond a mere monotonous swing, like the ticking of a pendulum; and the regular tick of the Equilateral is no less admired and copied by the wife of the progressive and aspiring Isosceles, in the females of whose family no" back-motion" of any kind has become as yet a necessity of life. Hence, in every family of position and consideration, "back motion" is as prevalent as time itself; and the husbands and sons in these households enjoy immunity at least from invisible attacks.

Not that it must be for a moment supposed that our Women are destitute of affection. But unfortunately the passion of the moment predominates, in the Frail Sex, over every other consideration. This is, of course, a necessity arising from their unfortunate conformation. For as they have no pretensions to an angle, being inferior in this respect to the very lowest of the, Isosceles, they are consequently wholly devoid of brain-power, and have neither reflection, judgment nor forethought, and hardly any memory. Hence, in their fits of fury, they remember no claims and recognize no distinctions. I have actually known a case where a Woman has exterminated her whole household, and half an hour afterwards, when her rage was over and the fragments swept away, has asked what has become of her husband and her children!

Obviously then a Woman is not to be irritated as long as she is in a position where she can turn round. When you have them in their apartments—which are constructed with a view to denying them that power—you can say and do what you like; for they are then wholly impotent for mischief, and will not remember a few minutes hence the incident for which they may be at this moment threatening you with death, nor the promises which you may have found it necessary to make in order to pacify their fury.

On the whole we get on pretty smoothly in our domestic relations, except in the lower strata of the Military Classes. There the want of tact and discretion on the part of the husbands produces at times indescribable disasters. Relying too much on the offensive weapons of their acute angles instead of the defensive organs of good sense and seasonable simulations, these reckless creatures too often neglect the prescribed construction of the Women's apartments, or irritate their wives by ill-advised expressions out of doors, which they refuse immediately to retract. Moreover a blunt and stolid regard for literal truth indisposes them to make those lavish promises by which the more judicious Circle can in a moment pacify his consort. The result is massacre; not however without its advantages, as it eliminates the more brutal and troublesome of the Isosceles; and by many of our Circles the destructiveness of the Thinner Sex is regarded as one among many providential arrangements for suppressing redundant population, and nipping Revolution in the bud.

Yet even in our best regulated and most approximately circular families I cannot say that the ideal of family life is so high as with you in Spaceland. There is peace, in so far as the absence of slaughter may be called by that name, but there is necessarily little harmony of tastes or pursuits; and the cautious wisdom of the Circles has ensured safety at the cost of domestic comfort. In every Circular or Polygonal household it has been a habit from time immemorial—and has now become a kind of instinct among the women of our higher classes—that the mothers and daughters should constantly keep their eyes and mouths towards their husband and his male friends; and for a lady in a family of distinction to turn her back upon her husband would be regarded as a kind of portent, involving loss of *status*. But, as I shall soon shew, this custom, though it has the advantage of safety, is not without its disadvantages.

In the house of the Working Man or respectable Tradesman—where the wife is allowed to turn her back upon her husband, while pursuing her household avocations—there are at least intervals of quiet, when the wife is neither seen nor heard, except for the humming sound of the continuous Peace-cry; but in the homes of the upper classes there is too often no peace. There the voluble mouth and bright penetrating eye are ever directed towards the Master of the household; and light itself is not more persistent than the stream of feminine discourse. The tact and skill which suffice to avert a Woman's sting are unequal to the task of stopping a Woman's mouth; and as the wife has absolutely nothing to say, and absolutely no constraint of wit, sense, or conscience to prevent her from saying it, not a few cynics have been found to aver that they prefer the danger of the death-dealing but inaudible sting to the safe sonorousness of a Woman's other end.

To my readers in Spaceland the condition of our Women may seem truly deplorable, and so indeed it is. A Male of the lowest type of the Isosceles may look forward to some improvement of his angle and to the ultimate elevation of the whole of his degraded caste; but no Woman can entertain such hopes for her sex. "Once a Woman, always a Woman" is a Decree of Nature; and the very Laws of Evolution seem suspended in her disfavor. Yet at least we can admire the wise Prearrangement which has ordained that, as they have no hopes, so they shall have no memory to recall, and no forethought to anticipate, the miseries and humiliations which are at once a necessity of their existence and the basis of the constitution of Flatland.

§ 5.—Of our methods of recognizing one another.

You, who are blessed with shade as well as light, you who are gifted with two eyes, endowed with a knowledge of perspective, and charmed with the enjoyment of various colors, you, who can actually *see* an angle, and contemplate the complete circumference of a Circle in the happy region of the Three Dimensions—how shall I make clear to you the extreme difficulty which we in Flatland experience in recognizing one another's configurations?

Recall what I told you above. All beings in Flatland, animate or inanimate, no matter what their form, present *to our view* the same, or nearly the same, appearance, viz. that of a straight Line. How then can one be distinguished from another, where all appear the same?

The answer is threefold. The first means of recognition is the sense of hearing; which with us is far more highly developed than with you, and which enables us not only to distinguish by the voice our personal friends, but even to discriminate between different classes, at least so far as concerns the three lowest orders, the Equilateral, the Square, and the Pentagon—for of the Isosceles I take no account. But as we ascend in the social scale, the process of discriminating and being discriminated by hearing increases in difficulty, partly because voices are assimilated, partly because the faculty of voice-discrimination is a plebeian virtue not much developed among the Aristocracy. And wherever there is any danger of imposture we cannot trust to this method. Amongst our lowest orders, the vocal organs are developed to a degree more than correspondent with those of hearing, so that an Isosceles can easily feign the voice of a Polygon, and, with some training, that of a Circle himself. A second method is therefore more commonly resorted to.

Feeling is, among our Women and lower classes—about our upper classes I shall speak presently—the principal test of recognition, at all events between strangers, and when the question is, not as to the individual, but as to the class. What therefore "introduction" is among the higher classes in Spaceland, that the process of "feeling" is with us. "Permit me to ask you to feel and be felt by my friend Mr. So-and-so"—is still, among the more old-fashioned of our country gentlemen in districts remote from towns, the customary formula for a Flatland introduction. But in the towns, and among men of business, the words "be felt by" are omitted and the sentence is abbreviated to, "Let me ask you to feel Mr. So-and-so"; although it is assumed, of course, that the "feeling" is to be reciprocal. Among our still more modern and dashing young gentlemen—who are extremely averse to superfluous effort and supremely indifferent to the purity of their native language—the formula is still further curtailed by the use of "to feel" in a technical sense, meaning, "to recommend-for-the purposes-of-feeling-and-being-felt"; and at this moment the "slang" of polite or fast society in the upper classes sanctions such a barbarism as "Mr. Smith, permit me to feel you Mr. Jones."

Let not my Reader however suppose that "feeling" is with us the tedious process that it would be with you, or that we find it necessary to feel right round all the sides of every individual before we determine the class to which he belongs. Long practice and training, begun in the schools and continued in the experience of daily life, enable us to discriminate at once by the sense of touch, between the angles of an equal-sided Triangle, Square, and Pentagon; and I need not say that the brainless vertex of an acute-angled Isosceles is obvious to the dullest touch. It is therefore not necessary, as a rule, to do more than feel a single angle of any individual; and this, once ascertained, tells us the class of the person whom we are addressing, unless indeed he belongs to the higher sections of the nobility. There the difficulty is much greater. Even a Master of Arts in our University of Wentbridge has been known to confuse a ten-sided with a twelve-sided Polygon; and there is hardly a Doctor of Science in or out of that famous University who could pretend to decide promptly and unhesitatingly between a twenty-sided and a twenty-four sided member of the Aristocracy.

Those of my readers who recall the extracts I gave above from the Legislative code concerning Women, will readily perceive that the process of introduction by contact requires some care and discretion. Otherwise the angles might inflict on the unwary Feeler irreparable injury. It is essential for the safety of the Feeler that the Felt should stand perfectly still. A start, a fidgety shifting of the position, yes, even a violent sneeze, has been known before now to prove fatal to the incautious, and to nip in the bud many a promising friendship. Especially is this true among the lower classes of the Triangles. With them, the eye is situated so far from their vertex that they can scarcely take cognizance of what goes on at that extremity of their frame. They are moreover of a rough coarse nature, not sensitive to the delicate touch of the highly organized Polygon. What wonder then if an involuntary toss of the head has ere now deprived the State of a valuable life!

I have heard that my excellent Grandfather—one of the least irregular of his unhappy Isosceles class, who indeed obtained, shortly before his decease, four out of seven votes from the Sanitary and Social Board for passing him into the class of the Equal-sided—often deplored with a tear in his venerable eye, a miscarriage of this kind, which had occurred to his great-great-great-Grand father, a respectable Working Man with an angle or brain of 59° 30'. According to his account, my unfortunate Ancestor, being afflicted with rheumatism, and in the act of being felt by a Polygon, by one sudden start accidentally transfixed the Great Man through the diagonal; and thereby, partly in consequence of his long imprisonment and degradation, and partly because of the moral shock which pervaded the whole of my Ancestor's relations, threw back our family a degree and a half in their ascent towards better things. The result was that in the next generation the family brain was registered at only 58°, and not till the lapse of five generations was the lost ground recovered, the full 60° attained, and the Ascent from the Isosceles finally achieved. And all this series of calamities from one little accident in the process of Feeling.

At this point I think I hear some of my better educated readers exclaim, "How could you in Flatland know anything about angles and degrees, or minutes? We can *see* an angle, because we in the region of Space, can see two straight lines inclined to one another; but you, who can see nothing but one straight line at a time, or at all events only a number of bits of straight lines all in one straight line,—how can you ever discern any angle, and much less register angles of different sizes?"

I answer that though we cannot *see* angles, we can *infer* them, and this with great precision. Our sense of touch, stimulated by necessity, and developed by long training, enables us to distinguish angles far more accurately than your sense of sight, when unaided by a rule or measure of angles. Nor must I omit to explain that we have great natural helps. It is with us a Law of Nature that the brain of the Isosceles class shall begin at half a degree, or thirty minutes, and shall increase (if it increases at all) by half a degree in every generation; until the goal of 60° is reached, when the condition of serfdom is quitted, and the freeman enters the class of Regulars.

Consequently, Nature herself supplies us with an ascending scale or Alphabet of angles for half a degree up to 60°, Specimens of which are placed in every Elementary School throughout the land. Owing to occasional retrogressions, to still more frequent moral and intellectual stagnation, and to the extraordinary fecundity of the Criminal and Vagabond Classes, there is always a vast superfluity of individuals of the half degree and single degree class, and a fair abundance of Specimens up to 10°. These are absolutely destitute of civic rights; and a great number of them, not having even intelligence enough for the purposes of warfare, are devoted by the States to the service of education. Fettered immovably so as to remove all possibility of danger, they are placed in the class rooms of our Infant Schools, and there they are utilized by the Board of Education for the purpose of imparting to the offspring of the Middle Classes that tact and intelligence of which these wretched creatures themselves are utterly devoid.

In some states the Specimens are occasionally fed and suffered to exist for several years; but in the more temperate and better regulated regions, it is found in the long run more advantageous for the educational interests of the young, to dispense with food, and to renew the Specimens every month,—which is about the average duration of the foodless existence of the Criminal class. In the cheaper schools, what is gained by the longer existence of the Specimens is lost, partly in the expenditure for food, and partly in the diminished accuracy of the angles, which are impaired after a few weeks of constant "feeling." Nor must we forget to add, in enumerating the advantages of the more expensive system, that it tends, though slightly yet perceptibly, to the diminution of the redundant Isosceles population—an object which every statesman in Flatland constantly keeps in view. On the whole therefore—although I am not ignorant that, in many popularly elected School Boards, there is a reaction in favor of "the cheap system," as it is called—I am myself disposed to think that this is one of the many cases in which expense is the truest economy.

But I must not allow questions of School Board politics to divert me from my subject. Enough has been said, I trust, to show that Recognition by Feeling is not so tedious or indecisive a process as might have been supposed; and it is obviously more trustworthy than Recognition by hearing. Still there remain, as has been pointed out above, the objection that this method is not without danger.' For this reason many in the Middle and Lower classes, and all without exception in the Polygonal and Circular orders, prefer a third method, the description of which shall be reserved for the next section.

§ 6.—Of Recognition by Sight.

I am about to appear very inconsistent. In previous sections I have said that all figures in Flatland present the appearance of a straight line; and it was added or implied, that it is consequently impossible to distinguish by the visual organ between individuals of different classes: yet now I am about to explain to my Spaceland Critics how we are able to recognize one another by the sense of sight.

If however the Reader will take the trouble to refer to the passage in which Recognition by Feeling is stated to be universal, he will find this qualification—"among the lower classes." It is only among the higher classes and in our more temperate climates that Sight Recognition is practiced.

That this power exists in any regions and for any classes, is the result of Fog; which prevails during the greater part of the year in all parts save the torrid zones. That which is with you in Spaceland an unmixed evil, blotting out the landscape, depressing the spirits, and enfeebling the health, is by us recognized as a blessing scarcely inferior to air itself, and as the Nurse of arts and Parent of sciences. But let me explain my meaning, without further eulogies on this beneficent Element.

If Fog were non-existent, all lines would appear equally and in-distinguishably clear; and this is actually the case in those unhappy countries in which the atmosphere is perfectly dry and transparent.But wherever there is a rich supply of Fog, objects that are at a distance, say of three feet, are appreciably dimmer than those at a distance of two feet eleven inches; and the result is that by careful and constant experimental observation of comparative dimness and clearness, we are enabled to infer with great exactness the configuration of the object observed.

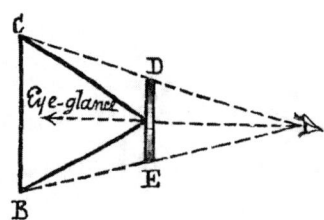

An instance will do more than a volume of generalities to make my meaning clear.

Suppose I see two individuals approaching whose rank I wish to ascertain. They are, we will suppose, a Merchant and a Physician, or in other words, an Equilateral Triangle and a Pentagon: how am I to distinguish them?

It will be obvious, to every child in Spaceland who has touched the threshold of Geometrical Studies, that, if I can bring my eye so that its glance may bisect an angle (A) of the approaching stranger, my view will lie as it were evenly between his two sides that are next to me (viz. CA and AB), so that I shall contemplate the two impartially, and both will appear of the same size.

Now in the case of (i) the Merchant, what shall I see? I shall see a straight line DAE, in which the middle point (A) will be very bright because it is nearest to me; but on either side the line will shade away *rapidly into dimness*, because the sides AC and AD *recede rapidly into the fog*; and what appear to me as the Merchant's extremities, viz. D and C, will be *very dim indeed*.

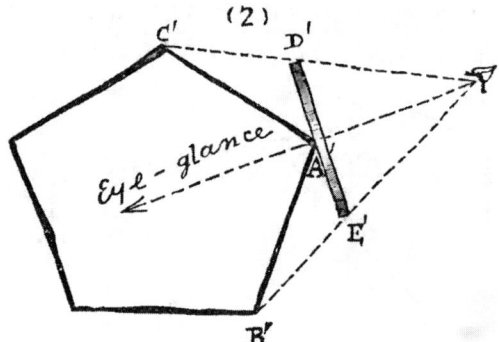

On the other hand in the case of (2) the Physician, though I shall here also see a line (D'A'E) with a bright centre (A'), yet it will shade away less *rapidly* into dimness, because the sides (A'C', A'B') *recede less rapidly into the fog*; and what appear to me the Physician's extremities, viz. D' and E', will be *not so dim* as the extremities of the Merchant.

The Reader will probably understand from these two instances how —after a very long training supplemented by constant experience—it is possible for the well-educated classes among us to discriminate with fair accuracy between the middle and lowest orders, by the sense of sight. If my Spaceland Patrons have grasped this general conception, so far as to conceive the possibility of it and not to reject my account as altogether incredible—I shall have attained all I can reasonably expect. Were I to attempt further details I should only perplex. Yet for the sake of the young and inexperienced, who may perchance infer—from the two simple instances I have given above, of the manner in which I should recognize my Father and my Sons—that Recognition by sight is an easy affair, it may be needful to point out that in actual life most of the problems of Sight Recognition are far more subtle and complex.

If for example, when my Father, the Triangle, approaches me, he happens to present his side to me instead of his angle, then, until I have asked him to rotate, or until I have edged my eye round him, I am for the moment doubtful whether he may not be a Straight Line, or, in other words, a Woman. Again, when I am in the company of one of my two hexagonal Grandsons, contemplating one of his sides (AB) full front, it will be evident from the accompanying diagram that I shall see one whole line (AB) in comparative brightness (shading off hardly at all at the ends) and two smaller lines (CA and BD) dim throughout and shading away into greater dimness toward the extremities C and D.

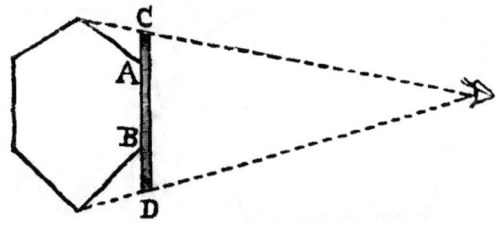

But I must not give way to the temptation of enlarging on these topics. The meanest mathematician in Spaceland will readily believe me when I assert that the problems of life, which present themselves to the well-educated—when they are themselves in motion, rotating, advancing or retreating, and at the same time attempting to discriminate by the sense of sight between a number of Polygons of high rank moving in different directions, as for example in a ball-room or conversazione— must be of a nature to task the angularity of the most intellectual, and amply justify the rich endowments of the Learned Professors of Geometry, both Static and Kinetic, in the illustrious University of Wentbridge, where the Science and Art of Sight Recognition are regularly taught to large classes of the *elite* of the States.

It is only a few of the scions of our noblest and wealthiest houses, who are able to give the time and money necessary for the thorough prosecution of this noble and valuable Art. Even to me, a Mathematician of no mean standing, and the Grandfather of two most hopeful and perfectly regular Hexagons, to find myself in the midst of a crowd of rotating Polygons of the higher classes, is occasionally very perplexing. And of course to a common Tradesman, or Serf, such a sight is almost as unintelligible as it would be to you, my Reader, were you suddenly transported into our country.

In such a crowd you could see on all sides of you nothing but a Line, apparently straight, but of which the parts would vary irregularly and perpetually in brightness or dimness. Even if you had completed your third year in the Pentagonal and Hexagonal classes in the University, and were perfect in the theory of the subject, you would still find that there was need of many years of experience, before you could move in a fashionable crowd without jostling against your betters, whom it is against etiquette to ask to "feel," and who, by their superior culture and breeding, know all about your movements, while you know very little or nothing about theirs. In a word, to comport oneself with perfect propriety in Polygonal society, one ought to be a Polygon oneself. Such at least is the painful teaching of my experience.

It is astonishing how much the Art—or I may almost call it instinct— of Sight Recognition is developed by the habitual practice of it and by the avoidance of the custom of "Feeling." Just as, with you, the deaf and dumb, if once allowed to gesticulate and to use the hand-alphabet, will never acquire the more difficult but far more valuable art of lip-speech and lip-reading, so it is with us as regards "Seeing" and "Feeling." None who in early life resort to "Feeling" will ever learn "Seeing" in perfection.

For this reason, among our Higher Classes, "Feeling" is discouraged or absolutely forbidden. From the cradle their children, instead of going to the Public Elementary schools (where the art of Feeling is taught,) are sent to higher Seminaries of an exclusive character; and at our illustrious University, to "feel" is regarded as a most serious fault, involving Rustication for the first offence, and Expulsion for the second.

But among the lower classes the art of Sight Recognition is regarded as an unattainable luxury. A common Tradesman cannot afford to let his son spend a third of his life in abstract studies. The children of the poor are therefore allowed to "feel" from their earliest years, and they gain thereby a precocity and an early vivacity which contrast at first most favorably with the inert, undeveloped, and listless behavior of the half-instructed youths of the Polygonal class; but when the latter have at last completed their University course, and are prepared to put their theory into practice, the change that comes over them may almost be described as a new birth, and in every art, science, and social pursuit they rapidly overtake and distance their Triangular competitors.

Only a few of the Polygonal Class fail to pass the Final Test or Leaving Examination at the University. The condition of the unsuccessful minority is truly pitiable. Rejected from the higher class, they are also despised by the lower. They have neither the matured and systematically trained powers of the Polygonal Bachelors and Masters of Arts, nor yet the native precocity and mercurial versatility of the youthful Tradesman. The professions, the public services are closed against them; and though in most States they are not actually debarred from marriage, yet they have the greatest difficulty in forming suitable alliances, as experience shows that the offspring of such unfortunate and ill-endowed parents is generally itself unfortunate, if not positively Irregular.

It is from these specimens of the refuse of our Nobility that the great Tumults and Seditions of past ages have generally derived their leaders; and so great is the mischief thence arising that an increasing minority of our more progressive Statesmen are of opinion that true mercy would dictate their entire suppression, by enacting that all who fail to pass the Final Examination of the University should be either imprisoned for life, or extinguished by a painless death.

But I find myself digressing into the subject of Irregularities, a matter of such vital interest that it demands a separate section.

§ 7.—Of Irregular Figures.

Throughout the previous pages I have been assuming—what perhaps should have been laid down at the beginning as a distinct and fundamental proposition—that every human being in Flatland is a Regular Figure, that is to say of regular construction. By this I mean that a Woman must not only be a line, but a straight line; that an Artisan or Soldier must have two of his sides equal; that Tradesmen must have three sides equal; Lawyers (of which class I am a humble member), four sides equal, and, generally, that in every Polygon, all the sides must be equal.

The size of the sides would of course depend upon the age of the individual. A Female at birth would be about an inch long, while a tall adult Woman might extend to a foot. As to the Males of every class, it may be roughly said that the length of an adult's sides, when added together, is three feet or a little more. But the size of our sides is not under consideration. I am speaking of the *equality* of sides, and it does not need "much reflection to see that the whole of the social life in Flatland rests upon the fundamental fact that Nature wills all Figures to have their sides equal.

If our sides were unequal our angles would be unequal. Instead of its being sufficient to feel, or estimate by sight, a single angle in order to determine the form of an individual, it would be necessary to ascertain each angle by the experiment of Feeling. But life would be too short for such a tedious groping. The whole science and art of Sight Recognition would at once perish; Feeling, so far as it is an art, would not long survive; intercourse would become perilous or impossible; there would be an end to all confidence, all forethought; no one would be safe in making the most simple social arrangements; in a word, civilization would relapse into barbarism.

Am I going too fast to carry my Readers with me to these obvious conclusions? Surely a moment's reflection, and a single instance from common life, must convince everyone that our whole social system is based upon Regularity, or Equality of Angles. You meet, for example, two or three

Tradesmen in the street, whom you recognize at once to be Tradesmen by a glance at their angles and rapidly bedimmed sides, and you ask them to step into your house to lunch. This you do at present with perfect confidence, because everyone knows to an inch or two the area occupied by an adult Triangle: but imagine that your Tradesman drags behind his regular and respectable vertex, a parallelogram of twelve or thirteen inches in diagonal:—what are you to do with such a monster sticking fast in your house door?

But I am insulting the intelligence of my Readers by accumulating details which must be patent to everyone who enjoys the advantages of a Residence in Spaceland. Obviously the measurements of a single angle would no longer be sufficient under such portentous circumstances; one's whole life would be taken up in feeling or surveying the perimeter of one's acquaintances. Already the difficulties of avoiding a collision in a crowd are enough to tax the sagacity of even a well-educated Square; but if no one could calculate the Regularity of a single figure in the company, all would be chaos and confusion, and the slightest panic would cause serious injuries, or—if there happened to be any Women or Soldiers present— perhaps considerable loss of life.

Expediency therefore concurs with Nature in stamping the seal of its approval upon Regularity of conformation: nor has the Law been backward in seconding their efforts. "Irregularity of Figure" means with us the same as, or more than, a combination of moral obliquity and criminality with you, and is treated accordingly. There are not wanting, it is true, some promulgators of paradoxes who maintain that there is no necessary connection between geometrical and moral Irregularity. "The Irregular," they say, "is from his birth scouted by his own parents, derided by his brothers and sisters, neglected by the domestics, scorned and suspected by society, and excluded from all posts of responsibility, trust, and useful activity. His every movement is jealously watched by the police till he comes of age and presents himself for inspection; then he is either destroyed, if he is found to exceed the fixed margin of deviation, or else immured in a Government Office as a clerk of the seventh class; prevented from marriage; forced to drudge at an uninteresting occupation for a miserable stipend; obliged to live and board at the office, and to take even his vacation under close supervision; what wonder that human nature, even in the best and purest, is embittered and perverted by such surroundings!"

All this very plausible reasoning does not convince me, as it has not convinced the wisest of our Statesmen, that our ancestors erred in laying it down as an axiom of policy that the toleration of Irregularity is incompatible with the safety of the State. Doubtless, the life of an Irregular is hard; but the interests of the Greater Number require that it shall be hard. If a man with a triangular front and a polygonal back were allowed to exist and to propagate a still more Irregular posterity, what would become of the arts of life? Are the houses and doors and churches in Flatland to be altered in order to accommodate such monsters? Are our ticket-collectors to be required to measure every man's perimeter before they allow him to enter a theatre, or to take his place in a lecture room? Is an Irregular to be exempted from the militia? And if not, how is he to be prevented from carrying desolation into the ranks of his comrades? Again, what irresistible temptations to fraudulent impostures must needs beset such a creature! How easy for him to enter a shop with his polygonal front foremost, and to order goods to any extent from a confiding tradesman! Let the advocates of a falsely called Philanthropy plead as they may for the abrogation of the Irregular Penal Laws, I for my part have never known an Irregular who was not also what Nature evidently intended him to be—a hypocrite, a misanthropist, and, up to the limits of his power—a perpetrator of all manner of mischief.

Not that I should be disposed to recommend (at present) the extreme measures adopted in some States, where an infant whose angle deviates by half a degree from the correct angularity is summarily destroyed at birth. Some of our highest and ablest men, men of real genius, have during their earliest days labored under deviations as great as, or even greater than, forty-five minutes: and the loss of their precious lives would have been an irreparable injury to the State. The art of healing also has achieved some of its most glorious triumphs in the compressions, extensions, trepannings, colligations, and other surgical or diaetetic operations by which Irregularity has been partly or wholly cured. Advocating therefore a *Via Media*, I would lay down no fixed or absolute line of demarcation; but at the period when the frame is just beginning to set, and when the Medical Board has reported that recovery is improbable, I would suggest that the Irregular offspring be painlessly and mercifully consumed.

§ 8.—Of the Ancient Practice of Painting.

If my Readers have followed me with any attention up to this point, they will not be surprised to hear that life is somewhat dull in Flatland. I do not, of course, mean that there are not battles, conspiracies, tumults, factions, and all those other phenomena which are supposed to make History interesting; nor would I deny that the strange mixture of the problems of life and the problems of Mathematics, continually inducing conjecture and giving the opportunity of immediate verification, imparts to our existence a zest which you in Spaceland can hardly comprehend. I speak now from the aesthetic and artistic point of view when I say that life with us is dull; aesthetically and artistically, very dull indeed.

How can it be otherwise, when all one's prospect, all one's landscapes, historical pieces, portraits, flowers, still life, are nothing but a single line, with no varieties except degrees of brightness and obscurity?

It was not always thus. Color, if Tradition speaks the truth, once for the space of half a dozen centuries or more, threw a transient charm upon the lives of our ancestors in the remotest ages. Some private individual —a Pentagon whose name is variously reported—having casually discovered the constituents of the simpler colors and a rudimentary method of painting, is said to have begun by decorating first his house, then his slaves, then his Father, his Sons and Grandsons, lastly himself. The convenience as well as the beauty of the results commended themselves to all. Wherever Chromatistes,—for by that name the most trustworthy authorities concur in calling him,—turned his variegated frame, there he at once excited attention, and attracted respect. No one now needed to "feel" him; no one mistook his front for his back; all his movements were readily ascertained by his neighbors without the slightest strain on their powers of calculation; no one jostled him, or failed to make way for him; his voice was saved the labor of that exhausting utterance by which we colorless Squares and Pentagons are often forced to proclaim our individuality when we move amid a crowd of ignorant Isosceles.

The fashion spread like wildfire. Before a week was over, every Square and Triangle in the district had copied the example of Chromatistes, and only a few of the more conservative Pentagons still held out. A month or two found even the Dodecagons infected with the innovation. A year had not elapsed before the habit had spread to all but the very highest of the Nobility. Needless to say, the custom soon made its way from the district of Chromatistes to surrounding regions; and within two generations no one in all Flatland was colorless except the Women and the Priests.

Here Nature herself appeared to erect a barrier, and to plead against extending the innovation to these two classes. Many-sidedness was almost essential as a pretext for the Innovators. "Distinction of sides is intended by Nature to imply distinction of colors "—such was the sophism which in those days flew from mouth to mouth, converting whole towns at a time to the new culture. But manifestly to our Priests and Women this adage did not apply. The latter had only one side, and therefore—plurally and pedantically speaking— *no sides*. The former—if at least they would assert their claim to be really and truly Circles, and not mere high-class Polygons with an infinitely large number of infinitesimally small sides— were in the habit of boasting (what Women confessed and deplored) that they also had no sides, being blessed with a perimeter of one line or, in other words, a Circumference. Hence it came to pass that these two Classes could see no force in the so-called axiom about "Distinction of Sides implying Distinction of Color"; and when all others had succumbed to the fascinations of corporal decoration, the Priests and the Women alone still remained pure from the pollution of paint.

Immoral, licentious, anarchical, unscientific—call them by what names you will—yet, from an aesthetic point of view, those ancient days of the Color Revolt were the glorious childhood of Art in Flatland—a childhood, alas, that never ripened into manhood, nor even reached the blossom of youth. To live was then in itself a delight, because living implied seeing. Even at a small party, the company was a pleasure to behold; the richly varied hues of the assembly in a church or theatre are said to have more than once proved too distracting for our greatest teachers and actors; but most ravishing of all is said to have been the unspeakable magnificence of a military review.

The sight of a line of battle of twenty thousand Isosceles suddenly facing about, and exchanging the sombre black of their bases for the orange and purple of the two sides including their acute angle; the militia of the Equilateral Triangles tricolored in red, white, and blue; the mauve, ultramarine, gamboge, and burnt umber of the Square artillerymen rapidly rotating near their vermilion guns; the dashing and flashing of the five-colored and six-colored Pentagons and Hexagons careering across the field in their offices of surgeons, geometricians and aides-de-camp— all these may well have been sufficient to render credible the famous story how an illustrious Circle, overcome by the artistic beauty of the forces under his command, threw aside his marshal's baton and his royal crown, exclaiming that he henceforth exchanged them for the artist's pencil. How great and glorious the sensuous development of these days must have been is in part indicated by the very language and vocabulary of the period.

The commonest utterances of the commonest citizens in the time of the Colour Revolt seem to have been suffused with a richer tinge of word or thought; and to that era we are even now indebted for our finest poetry and for whatever rhythm still remains in the more scientific utterance of these modern days.

§ 9.—Of the Universal Color Bill.

But meanwhile the intellectual Arts were fast decaying.

The Art of Sight Recognition, being no longer needed, was no longer practiced; and the studies of Geometry, Statics, Kinetics, and other kindred subjects, came soon to be considered superfluous, and fell into disrepute and neglect even at our University. The inferior Art of Feeling speedily experienced the same fate at our Elementary Schools. Then the Isosceles classes, asserting that the Specimens were no longer used nor needed, and refusing to pay the customary tribute from the Criminal classes to the service of Education, waxed daily more numerous and more insolent on the strength of their immunity from the old burden which had formerly exercised the twofold wholesome effect of at once taming their brutal nature and thinning their excessive numbers.

Year by year the Soldiers and Artisans began more vehemently to assert—and with increasing truth—that there was no great difference between them and the very highest class of Polygons, now that they were raised to an equality with the latter, and enabled to grapple with all the difficulties and solve all the problems of life, whether Statical and Kinetical, by the simple process of Color Recognition. Not content with the natural neglect into which Sight Recognition was falling, they began boldly to demand the legal prohibition of all "monopolizing and aristocratic Arts" and the consequent abolition of all endowments for the studies of Sight Recognition, Mathematics, and Feeling. Soon, they began to insist that inasmuch as Color, which was a second Nature, had destroyed the need of aristocratic distinctions, the Law should follow in the same path, and that henceforth all individuals and all classes should be recognized as absolutely equal and entitled to equal rights.

Finding the higher Orders wavering and undecided, the leaders of the Revolution advanced still further in their requirements, and at last demanded that all classes alike, the Priests and the Women not excepted, should do homage to Color by submitting to be painted. When it was objected that Priests and Women had no sides, they retorted that Nature and Expediency concurred in dictating that the front half of every human being (that is to say, the half containing his eye and mouth) should be distinguishable from his hinder half. They therefore brought before a general and extraordinary Assembly of all the States of Flatland a Bill proposing that in every Woman the half containing the eye and mouth should be colored red, and the other half green. The Priests were to be painted in the same way, red being applied to that semicircle in which the eye and mouth formed the middle point; while the other or hinder semicircle was to be colored green.

There was no little cunning in this proposal, which indeed emanated, not from any Isosceles —for no being so degraded would have had angularity enough to appreciate, much less to devise, such a model of state-craft—but from an Irregular Circle who, instead of being destroyed in his childhood, was reserved by a foolish indulgence to bring desolation on his country and destruction on myriads of his followers.

On the one hand the proposition was calculated to bring the Women in all classes over to the side of the Chromatic Innovation. For by assigning to the Women the same two colors as were assigned to the Priests, the Revolutionists thereby ensured that, in certain positions, every Woman would appear like a Priest, and be treated with corresponding respect and deference—a prospect that could not fail to attract the Female Sex in a mass.

But by some of my Readers the possibility of the identical appearance of Priests and Women, under the new Legislation, may not be recognized; if so, a word or two will make it obvious.

Imagine a woman duly decorated, according to the new Code; with the front half (*i.e.* the half containing eye and mouth) red, and with the hinder half green. Look at her from one side. Obviously you will see a straight line, *half red, half green*.

Now imagine a Priest, whose mouth is at M, and whose front semicircle (AMB) is consequently colored red, while his hinder semicircle is green; so that the diameter AB divides the green from the red. If you contemplate the Great Man so as to have your eye in the same straight line as his dividing diameter (AB), what you will see will be a straight line (CBD), of which *one half* (CB) *will be red, and the other* (BD) *green.* The whole line (CD) will be rather shorter perhaps than that of a full-sized Woman, and will shade off more rapidly towards its extremities; but the identity of the colors would give you an immediate impression of identity if not Class, making you neglectful of other details. Bear in mind the decay of Sight Recognition which threatened society at the time of the Color Revolt; add too the certainty that Women would speedily learn to shade off their extremities so as to imitate the Circles; it must then be surely obvious to you, my dear Reader, that the Color Bill placed us under a great danger of confounding a Priest with a young Woman.

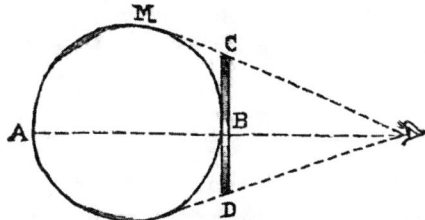

How attractive this prospect must have been to the Frail Sex may readily be imagined. They anticipated with delight the confusion that would ensue.

At home they might hear political and ecclesiastical secrets intended not for them but for their husbands and brothers, and might even issue commands in the name of a priestly Circle; out of doors the striking combination of red and green, without addition of any other colors, would be sure to lead the common people into endless mistakes, and the Women would gain whatever the Circles lost, in the deference of the passers by. As for the scandal that would befall the Circular Class if the frivolous and unseemly conduct of the Women were imputed to them, and as to the consequent subversion of the Constitution, the Female Sex could not be expected to give a thought to these considerations. Even in the households of the Circles, the Women were all in favor of the Universal Color Bill.

The second object aimed at by the Bill was the gradual demoralization of the Circles themselves. In the general intellectual decay they still preserved their pristine clearness and strength of understanding. From their earliest childhood, familiarized in their Circular households with the total absence of Color, the Nobles alone preserved the Sacred Art of Sight Recognition, with all the advantages that result from that admirable training of the intellect. Hence, up to the date of the introduction of the Universal Color Bill, the Circles had not only held their own, but even increased their lead of other classes by abstinence from the popular fashion.

Now therefore the artful Irregular whom I described above as the real author of this diabolical Bill, determined at one blow to lower the status of the Hierarchy by forcing them to submit to the pollution of Color, and at the same time to destroy their domestic opportunities of training in the Art of Sight Recognition, so as to enfeeble their intellects by depriving them of their pure and colorless homes. Once subjected to the chromatic taint, every parental and every childish Circle would demoralize each other. Only in discerning between the Father and the Mother would the Circular infant find problems for the exercise of its understanding—problems too often likely to be corrupted by maternal impostures with the result of shaking the child's faith in all logical conclusions. Thus by degrees the intellectual lustre of the Priestly Order would wane, and the road would then lie open for a total destruction of all Aristocratic Legislature and for the subversion of our Privileged Classes.

§ 10.—Of the Suppression of the Chromatic Sedition.

The agitation for the Universal Color Bill continued for three years; and up to the last moment of that period it seemed as though Anarchy were destined to triumph.

A whole army of Polygons, who turned out to fight as private soldiers, was utterly annihilated by a superior force of Isosceles Triangles—the Squares and Pentagons meanwhile remaining neutral. Worse than all, some of the ablest Circles fell a prey to conjugal fury. Infuriated by political animosity, the wives in many a noble household wearied their lords with prayers to give up their opposition to the Color Bill; and some, finding their entreaties fruitless, fell on and slaughtered their innocent children and husbands, perishing themselves in the act of carnage. It is recorded that during that triennial agitation no less than twenty-three Circles perished in domestic discord.

Great indeed was the peril. It seemed as though the Priests had no choice between submission and extermination; when suddenly the course of events was completely changed by one of those picturesque incidents which Statesmen ought never to neglect, often to anticipate, and sometimes perhaps to originate, because of the absurdly disproportionate power with which they appeal to the sympathies of the populace.

It happened that an Isosceles of a low type, with a brain little if at all above four degrees—accidentally dabbling in the colors of some Tradesman whose shop he had plundered—painted himself, or caused himself to be painted (for the story varies) with the twelve colors of a Dodecahedron. Going into the Market Place he accosted in a feigned voice a maiden, the orphan daughter of a noble Polygon, whose affection in former days he had sought in vain; and by a series of deceptions, aided on the one side by a string of lucky accidents too long to relate, and, on the other, by an almost inconceivable fatuity and neglect of ordinary precautions on the part of the relations of the bride, he succeeded in consummating the marriage. The unhappy girl committed suicide on discovering the fraud to which she had been subjected.

When the news of this catastrophe spread from State to State the minds of the Women were violently agitated. Sympathy with the miserable victim and anticipations of similar deceptions for themselves, their sisters, and their daughters, made them now regard the Color Bill in an entirely new aspect. Not a few openly avowed themselves converted to antagonism; the rest needed only a slight stimulus to make a similar avowal. Seizing this favorable opportunity the Circles hastily convened an extraordinary Assembly of the States; and besides the usual guard of Convicts, they secured the attendance of a large number of reactionary Women.

Amidst an unprecedented concourse, the Chief Circle of those days—by name Pantocyclus—arose to find himself hissed and hooted by a hundred and twenty thousand Isosceles. But he secured silence by declaring that henceforth the Circles would enter on a policy of Concession; yielding to the wishes of the majority, they would accept the Color Bill. The uproar being at once converted to applause, he invited Chromatistes, the leader of the Sedition, into the centre of the hall, to receive in the name of his followers the submission of the Hierarchy. Then followed a speech, a masterpiece of rhetoric, which occupied nearly a day in the delivery, and to which no summary can do justice.

With a grave appearance of impartiality he declared that as they were now finally committing themselves to Reform or Innovation, it was desirable that they should take one last view of the perimeter of the whole subject, its defects as well as its advantages. Gradually introducing the mention of the dangers to the Tradesmen, the Professional Classes and the Gentlemen, he silenced the rising murmurs of the Isosceles by reminding them that, in spite of all these defects, he was willing to accept the Bill if it was approved by the majority. But it was manifest that all, except the Isosceles, were moved by his words and were either neutral or averse to the Bill.

Turning now to the Workmen he asserted that their interests must not be neglected, and that, if they intended to accept the Color Bill, they ought at least to do so with a full view of the consequences. Many of them, he said, were on the point of being admitted to the class of the Regular Triangles; others anticipated for their children a distinction they could not hope for themselves.

That honorable ambition would now have to be sacrificed. With the universal adoption of Color, all distinctions would cease; Regularity would be confused with Irregularity; development would give place to retrogression; the Workman would in a few generations be degraded to the level of the Military, or even the Convict Class; political power would be in the hands of the greatest number, that is to say the Criminal Classes, who were already more numerous than the Workmen, and would soon out-number all the other Classes put together when the usual Compensative Laws of Nature were violated.

A subdued murmur of assent ran through the ranks of the Artisans, and Chromatistes, in alarm, attempted to step forward and address them. But he found himself encompassed with guards and forced to remain silent while the Chief Circle in a few impassioned words made a final appeal to the Women, exclaiming that, if the Color Bill passed, no marriage would henceforth be safe, no woman's honor secure; fraud, deception, hypocrisy would pervade every household; domestic bliss would share the fate of the Constitution and pass to speedy perdition. Sooner than this, he cried "Come death."

At these words, which were the preconcerted signal for action, the Isosceles Convicts fell on and transfixed the wretched Chromatistes; the Regular Classes opening their ranks, made way for a band of Women who, under direction of the Circles, moved, back foremost, invisibly and unerringly upon the unconscious Soldiers; the Artisans, imitating the example of their betters, also opened their ranks. Meantime bands of Convicts occupied every entrance with an impenetrable phalanx.

The battle, or rather carnage, was of short duration. Under the skilful generalship of the Circles almost every Woman's charge was fatal, and very many extracted their sting uninjured, ready for a second slaughter. But no second blow was needed; the rabble of the Isosceles did the rest of the business for themselves. Surprised, leader-less, attacked in front by invisible foes, and finding egress cut off by the Convicts behind them, they at once—after their manner— lost all presence of mind, and raised the cry of "treachery." This sealed their fate. Every Isosceles now saw and felt a foe in every other. In half an hour not one of that vast multitude was living; and the fragments of seven score thousand of the Criminal Class slain by one another's angles attested the triumph of Order.

The Circles delayed not to push their victory to the uttermost. The Working Men they spared but decimated. The Militia of the Equilaterals was at once called out; and every Triangle suspected of Irregularity on reasonable grounds, was destroyed by Court Martial, without the formality of exact measurement by the Social Board. The homes of the Military and Artisan classes were inspected in a course of visitations extending through upwards of a year; and during that period every town, village, and hamlet was systematically purged of that excess of the lower orders which had been brought about by the neglect to pay the Tribute of Criminals to the Schools and University, and by the violation of the other natural Laws of the Constitution of Flatland. Thus the balance of classes was again restored.

Needless to say that henceforth the use of Color was abolished, and its possession prohibited. Even the utterance of any word denoting Color, except by the Circles or by qualified scientific teachers, was punished by a severe penalty. Only at our University in some of the very highest and most esoteric classes— which I myself have never been privileged to attend—it is understood that the sparing use of Color is still sanctioned for the purpose of illustrating some of the deeper problems of mathematics. But of this I can only speak from hearsay.

Elsewhere in Flatland, Color is now non-existent. The art of making it is known to only one living person, the Chief Circle for the time being; and by him it is handed down on his death-bed to none but his Successor. One manufactory alone produces it; and, lest the secret should be betrayed, the Workmen are annually consumed, and fresh ones introduced. So great is the terror with which even now our Aristocracy looks back to the far-distant days of the agitation for the Universal Color Bill.

§ 11.—Concerning our Priests.

It is high time that I should pass from these brief and discursive notes about things in Flatland to the central event of this book, my initiation into the mysteries of Space. *That* is my subject; all that has gone before is merely preface.

For this reason I must omit many matters of which the explanation would not, I flatter myself, be without interest for my Readers: as for example, our method of propelling and stopping ourselves, although destitute of feet; the means by which we give fixity to structures of wood, stone, or brick, although of course we have no hands, nor can we lay foundations as you can, nor avail ourselves of the lateral pressure of the earth; the manner in which the rain originates in the intervals between our various zones, so that the northern regions do not intercept the moisture from falling on the southern; the nature of our hills and mines, our trees and vegetables, our seasons and harvests; our Alphabet, and method of writing, adapted to our linear tablets; these and a hundred other details of our physical existence I must pass over, nor do I mention them now except to indicate to my readers that their omission proceeds not from forgetfulness on the part of the Author, but from his regard for the time of the Reader.

Yet before I proceed to my legitimate subject some few final remarks will no doubt be expected by my Readers upon those pillars and mainstays of the Constitution of Flatland, the controllers of our conduct and shapers of our destiny, the objects of universal homage and almost of adoration: need I say that I mean our Circles or Priests?

When I call them Priests, let me not be understood as meaning no more than the term denotes with you. With us, our Priests are Administrators of all Business, Art, and Science; Directors of Trade, Commerce, Generalship, Architecture, Engineering, Education, Statesmanship, Legislature, Morality, Theology; doing nothing themselves, they are the Causes of everything, worth doing, that is done by others.

Although popularly every one called a Circle is deemed a Circle, yet among the better educated Classes it is known that no Circle is really a Circle, but only a Polygon with a very large number of very small sides. In proportion to the number of the sides the Polygon approximates to a Circle; and, when the number is very great, say for example three or four hundred, it is extremely difficult for the most delicate touch to feel any polygonal angles. Let me say rather, it *would* be difficult: for, as I have shown above, Recognition by Feeling is unknown among the highest society, and to *feel* a Circle would be considered a most audacious insult. This habit of abstention from Feeling in the best society enables a Circle the more easily to sustain the veil of mystery in which, from his earliest years, he is wont to enwrap the exact nature of his Perimeter or Circumference. Three feet being the average Perimeter it follows that, in a Polygon of three hundred sides, each side will be no more than the hundredth part of a foot in length, or little more than the tenth part of an inch; and in a Polygon of six or seven hundred sides the sides are little larger than the diameter of a Spaceland pin-head. It is always assumed, by courtesy, that the Chief Circle for the time being has ten thousand sides.

The ascent of the posterity of the Circles in the social scale is not restricted, as it is among the lower Regular classes, by the Law of Nature which limits the increase of sides to one in each generation. If it were so, the number of sides in a Circle would be a mere question of pedigree and arithmetic, and the four hundred and ninety-seventh descendant of an Equilateral Triangle would necessarily be a Polygon with five hundred sides. But this is not the case. Nature's Law prescribes two antagonistic decrees affecting Circular propagation; first, that as the race climbs higher in the scale of development, so development shall proceed at an accelerated pace; second, that in the same proportion, the race shall become less fertile. Consequently in the home of a Polygon of four or five hundred sides it is rare to find a son; more than one is never seen. On the other hand the son of a five-hundred-sided Polygon has been known to possess five hundred and fifty, or even six hundred sides.

Art also steps in to help the process of the higher Evolution. Our physicians have discovered that the small and tender sides of an infant Polygon of the higher class can be fractured, and his whole frame re-set, with such exactness that a Polygon of two or three hundred sides sometimes—by no means always, for the process is attended with serious risk— but sometimes overleaps two or three hundred generations, and as it were doubles at a stroke, the number of his progenitors and the nobility of his descent.

Many a promising child is sacrificed in this way. Scarcely one out of ten survives. Yet so strong is the parental ambition among those Polygons who are, as it were, on the fringe of the Circular class, that it is very rare to find a Nobleman of that position in society, who has neglected to place his first-born son in the Circular Neo-Therapeutic Gymnasium before he has attained the age of a month.

One year determines success or failure. At the end of that time the child has, in all probability, added one more to the tombstones that crowd the Neo-Therapeutic Cemetery; but on rare occasions a glad procession bears back the little one to his exultant parents, no longer a Polygon, but a Circle, at least by courtesy: and a single instance of so blessed a result induces multitudes of Polygonal parents to submit to similar domestic sacrifices, which have a dissimilar issue.

§ 12.—Of the Doctrine of our Priests.

As to the doctrine of the Circles it may briefly be summed up in a single maxim, "Attend to your Configuration." Whether political, ecclesiastical, or moral, all their teaching has for its object the improvement of individual and collective Configuration—with special reference of course to the Configuration of the Circles, to which all other objects are subordinated.

It is the merit of the Circles that they have effectually suppressed those ancient heresies which led men to waste energy and sympathy in the vain belief that conduct depends upon will, effort, training, encouragement, praise, or anything else but Configuration. It was Pantocyclus—the illustrious Circle mentioned above, as the queller of the Color Revolt— who first convinced mankind that Configuration makes the man; that if, for example, you are born an Isosceles with two uneven sides, you will assuredly go wrong unless you have them made even—for which purpose you must go to the Isosceles Hospital; similarly, if you are a Triangle, or Square, or even a Polygon, born with any Irregularity, you must be taken to one of the Regular Hospitals to have your disease cured; otherwise you will end your days in the State Prison or by the angle of the State Executioner.

All faults or defects, from the slightest misconduct to the most flagitious crime, Pantocyclus attributed to some deviation from perfect Regularity in the bodily figure, caused perhaps (if not congenital) by some collision in a crowd; by neglect to take exercise, or by taking too much of it; or even by a sudden change of temperature, resulting in a shrinkage or expansion in some too susceptible part of the frame. Therefore, concluded that illustrious Philosopher, neither good conduct nor bad conduct is a fit subject, in any sober estimation, for either praise or blame. For why should you praise, for example, the integrity of a Square who faithfully defends the interests of his client, when you ought in reality rather to admire the exact precision of his Rectangles? Or again, why blame a lying, thievish Isosceles when you ought rather to deplore the incurable inequality of his sides?

Theoretically, this doctrine is unquestionable; but it has practical drawbacks. In dealing with an Isosceles, if a rascal pleads that he cannot help stealing because of his unevenness, you reply that for that very reason, because he cannot help being a nuisance to his neighbors, you, the Magistrate, cannot help sentencing him to be consumed—and there's an end of the matter. But in little domestic difficulties, where the penalty of consumption, or death, is out of the question, this theory of Configuration sometimes comes in awkwardly; and I must confess that occasionally when one of my own Hexagonal Grandsons pleads as an excuse for his disobedience that a sudden change of the temperature has been too much for his Perimeter, and that I ought to lay the blame not on him but on his Configuration, which can only be strengthened by abundance of the choicest sweetmeats, I neither see my way logically to reject, nor practically to accept, his conclusions.

For my own part, I find it best to assume that a good sound scolding or castigation has some latent and strengthening influence on my Grandson's Configuration; though I own that I have no grounds for thinking so. At all events I am not alone in my way of extricating myself from this dilemma; for I find that many of the highest Circles, sitting as Judges in Law courts, use praise and blame towards Regular and Irregular Figures; and in their homes I know by experience that, when scolding their children, they speak about "right" or "wrong" as vehemently and passionately as if they believed that these names represented real existences, and that a human Figure is really capable of choosing between them.

Consistently carrying out their policy of making Configuration the leading idea in every mind, the Circles reverse the nature of that Commandment which in Spaceland regulates the relations between parents and children. With you, children are taught to honor their parents; with us—next to the Circles, who are the chief object of universal homage—a man is taught to honor his Grandson, if he has one; or, if not, his Son. By "honor," however, is by no means meant "indulgence," but a reverent regard for their highest interests: and the Circles teach that the duty of fathers is to subordinate their own interests to those of posterity, thereby advancing the welfare of the whole State as well as that of their own immediate descendants.

The weak point in the system of the Circles—if a humble Square may venture to speak of anything Circular as containing any element of weakness—appears to me to be found in their relations with Women.

As it is of the utmost importance for Society that Irregular births should be discouraged, it follows that no Woman who has any Irregularities in her ancestry is a fit partner for one who desires that his posterity should rise by regular degrees in the social scale.

Now the Irregularity of a Male is a matter of measurement; but as all Women are straight, and therefore visibly Regular so to speak, one has to devise some other means of ascertaining what I may call their invisible Irregularity, that is to say their potential Irregularities as regards possible offspring. This is effected by carefully-kept pedigrees, which are preserved and supervised by the State; and without a certified pedigree no Woman is allowed to marry.

Now it might have been supposed that a Circle—proud of his ancestry and regardful for a posterity which might possibly issue hereafter in a Chief Circle— would be more careful than any other to choose a wife who had no blot on her escutcheon. But it is not so. The care in choosing a Regular wife appears to diminish as one rises in the social scale. Nothing would induce an aspiring Isosceles, who had hopes of generating an Equilateral Son, to take a wife who reckoned a single Irregularity among her Ancestors; a Square or Pentagon, who is confident that his family is steadily on the rise, does not enquire above the five-hundredth generation; a Hexagon or Dodecahedron is even more careless of the wife's pedigree; but a Circle has been known deliberately to take a wife who has had an Irregular Great-Grandfather, and all because of some slight superiority of lustre, or because of the charms of a low voice—which, with us, even more than with you, is thought "an excellent thing in Woman."

Such ill-judged marriages are, as might be expected, barren, if they do not result in positive Irregularity or in diminution of sides; but none of these evils have hitherto proved sufficiently deterrent. The loss of a few sides in a highly-developed Polygon is not easily noticed, and is sometimes compensated by a successful operation in the Neo-Therapeutic Gymnasium, as I have described above; and the Circles are too much disposed to acquiesce in infecundity as a

Law of the superior development. Yet, if this evil be not arrested, the gradual diminution of the Circular class may soon become more rapid, and the time may be not far distant when, the race being no longer able to produce a Chief Circle, the Constitution of Flatland must fall.

One other word of warning suggests itself to me, though I cannot so easily mention a remedy; and this also refers to our relations with Women. About three hundred years ago, it was decreed by the Chief Circle that, since women are deficient in Reason but abundant in Emotion, they ought no longer to be treated as rational, nor receive any mental education. The consequence was that they were no longer taught to read, nor even to master Arithmetic enough to enable them to count the angles of their husband or children; and hence they sensibly declined during each generation in intellectual power. And this system of female non-education or quietism still prevails.

My fear is that, with the best intentions, this policy has been carried so far as to react injuriously on the Male Sex.

For the consequence is that, as things now are, we Males have to lead a kind of bi-lingual, and I may almost say bi-mental existence. With the Women, we speak of "love," "duty," "right," "wrong," "pity," "hope," and other irrational and emotional conceptions, which have no existence, and the fiction of which has no object except to control feminine exuberances; but among ourselves, and in our books, we have an entirely different vocabulary and I may almost say, idiom. "Love" then becomes "the anticipation of benefits;", "duty" becomes "necessity" or "fitness;" and other words are correspondingly transmuted. Moreover, among Women, we use language implying the utmost deference for their Sex; and they fully believe that the Chief Circle Himself is not more devoutly adored by us than they are: but behind their backs they are both regarded and spoken of—by all except the very young—as being little better than "mindless organisms."

Our Theology also in the Women's chambers is entirely different from our Theology elsewhere.

Now my humble fear is that this double training, in language as well as in thought, imposes somewhat too heavy a burden upon the young, especially when, at the age of three years old, they are taken from the maternal care and taught to unlearn the old language—except for the purpose of repeating it in the presence of their Mothers and Nurses—and to learn the vocabulary and idiom of science. Already methinks I discern a weakness in the grasp of mathematical truth at the present time as compared with the more robust intellect of our ancestors three hundred years ago. I say nothing of the possible danger if a Woman should ever surreptitiously learn to read and convey to her Sex the result of her perusal of a single popular volume; nor of the possibility that the indiscretion or disobedience of some infant Male might reveal to a Mother the secrets of the logical dialect. On the simple ground of the enfeebling of the Male intellect, I rest this humble appeal to the highest Authorities to reconsider the regulations of Female Education.

PART II   OTHER WORLDS

"O brave new worlds,
That have such people in them!"

§ 1.—How I had a Vision of Lineland.

IT was the last day but one of the 1999th year of our era, and the first day of the Long Vacation. Having amused myself till a late hour with my favorite recreation of Geometry, I had retired to rest with an unsolved problem in my mind. In the night I had a dream.

I saw before me a vast multitude of small Straight Lines (which I naturally assumed to be Women) interspersed with other Beings still smaller and of the nature of lustrous Points—all moving to and fro in one and the same Straight Line, and, as nearly as I could judge, with the same velocity.

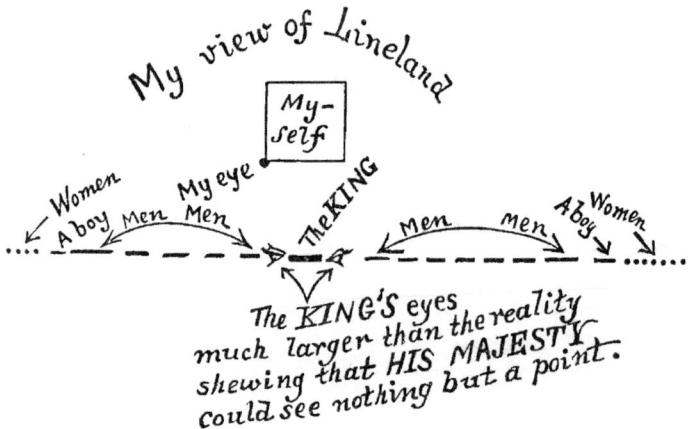

A noise of confused, multitudinous chirping or twittering issued from them at intervals as long as they were moving; but sometimes they ceased from motion, and then all was silence.

Approaching one of the largest of what I thought to be Women, I accosted her, but received no answer. A second and third appeal on my part were equally ineffectual. Losing patience at what appeared to me intolerable rudeness, I brought my mouth into a position full in front of her mouth so as to intercept her motion, and loudly repeated my question, "Woman, what signifies this concourse, and this strange and confused chirping, and this monotonous motion to and fro in one and the same Straight Line?"

"I am no Woman," replied the small Line; "I am the Monarch of the world. But thou, whence intrudest thou into my realm of Lineland?" Receiving this abrupt reply, I begged pardon if I had in any way startled or molested his Royal Highness; and describing myself as a stranger I besought the King to give me some account of his dominions. But I had the greatest possible difficulty in obtaining any information on points that really interested me; for the Monarch could not refrain from constantly assuming that whatever was familiar to him must also be known to me and that I was simulating ignorance in jest. However, by persevering questions I elicited the following facts:

It seemed that this poor ignorant Monarch—as he called himself—was persuaded that the Straight Line which he called his Kingdom, and in which he passed his existence, constituted the whole of the world, and indeed the whole of Space. Not being able either to move or to see, save in his Straight Line, he had no conception of anything out of it. Though he had heard my voice when I first addressed him, the sounds had come to him in a manner so contrary to his experience that he had made no answer, "seeing no man," as he expressed it, "and hearing a voice as it were from my own intestines." Until the moment when I placed my mouth in his World, he had neither seen me, nor heard anything except confused sounds beating against what I called his side, but what he called his *inside* or *stomach*; nor had he even now the least conception of the region from which I had come. Outside his World, or Line, all was a blank to him; nay, not even a blank, for a blank implies Space; say, rather, all was non-existent.

His subjects—of whom the small Lines were Men and the Points Women— were all alike confined in motion and eye-sight to that single Straight Line, which was their World. It need scarcely be added that the whole of their horizon was limited to a Point; nor could anyone ever see anything but a Point. Man, woman, child, thing—each was a Point to the eye of a Linelander. Only by the sound of the voice could sex or age be distinguished. Moreover, as each individual occupied the whole of the narrow path, so to speak, which constituted his Universe, and no one could move to the right or left to make way for passers by, it followed that no Linelander could ever pass another. Once neighbors, always neighbors. Neighborhood with them was like marriage with us.

Neighbors remained neighbors till death did them part.

Such a life, with all vision limited to a Point, and all motion to a Straight Line, seemed to me inexpressibly dreary; and I was surprised to note the vivacity and cheerfulness of the King. Wondering whether it was possible, amid circumstances so unfavorable to domestic relations, to enjoy the pleasures of conjugal union, I hesitated for some time to question his Royal Highness on so delicate a subject; but at last I plunged into it by abruptly inquiring as to the health of his family. "My wives and children," he replied, "are well and happy."

Staggered at this answer—for in the immediate proximity of the Monarch (as I had noted in my dream before I entered Lineland) there were none but Men— I ventured to reply, "Pardon me, but I cannot imagine how your Royal Highness can at any time either see or approach their Majesties, when there are at least half a dozen intervening individuals, whom you can neither see through, nor pass by? Is it possible that in Lineland proximity is not necessary for marriage and for the generation of children?"

"How can you ask so absurd a question?" replied the Monarch. "If it were indeed as you suggest, the Universe would soon be depopulated. No, no; neighborhood is needless for the union of hearts; and the birth of children is too important a matter to have been allowed to depend upon such an accident as proximity. You cannot be ignorant of this. Yet since you are pleased to affect ignorance, I will instruct you as if you were the veriest baby in Lineland. Know, then, that marriages are consummated by means of the faculty of sound and the sense of hearing."

"You are of course aware that every Man has two mouths or voices— as well as two eyes—a bass at one and a tenor at the other of his extremities. I should not mention this, but that I have been unable to distinguish your tenor in the course of our conversation." I replied that I had but one voice, and that I had not been aware that His Royal Highness had two." That confirms my impression," said the King, "that you are not a Man, but a feminine Monstrosity with a bass voice and an utterly uneducated ear. But to continue.

"Nature herself having ordained that every Man should wed two wives——"

"Why two?" asked I.

"You carry your affected simplicity too far," he cried.

"How can there be a completely harmonious union without the combination of the Four in One, viz. the Bass and Tenor of the Man and the Soprano and Contralto of the two Women?"

"But supposing," said I, "that a man should prefer one wife or three?"

"It is impossible," he said; "it is as inconceivable as that two and one should make five, or that the human eye should see a Straight Line." I would have interrupted him; but he proceeded as follows:

"Once in the middle of each week a Law of Nature compels us to move to and fro with a rhythmic motion of more than usual violence, which continues for the time you would take to count a hundred and one. In the midst of this choral dance, at the fifty-first pulsation, the inhabitants of the Universe pause in full career, and each individual sends forth his richest, fullest, sweetest strain. It is in this decisive moment that all our marriages are made. So exquisite is the adaptation of Bass to Treble, of Tenor to Contralto, that oftentimes the Loved Ones, though twenty thousand leagues away, recognize at once the responsive note of their destined Lover; and, penetrating the paltry obstacles of distance, Love unites the three. The marriage in that instant consummated results in a threefold Male and Female offspring which takes its place in Lineland."

"What! Always threefold?" said I. "Must one wife then always have twins?"

"Bass-voiced Monstrosity! Yes," replied the King. "How else could the balance of the Sexes be maintained, if two girls were not born for every boy? Would you ignore the very Alphabet of Nature?" He ceased, speechless for fury; and some time elapsed before I could induce him to resume his narrative.

"You will not, of course, suppose that every bachelor among us finds his mates at the first wooing in this universal Marriage Chorus. On the contrary, the process is by most of us many times repeated. Few are the hearts whose happy lot is at once to recognize in each other's voices the partner intended for them by Providence, and to fly into a reciprocal and perfectly harmonious embrace. With most of us the courtship is of long duration. The Wooer's voices may perhaps accord with one of the future wives, but not with both; or not, at first, with either; or the Soprano and Contralto may not quite harmonize. In such cases Nature has provided that every weekly Chorus shall bring the three Lovers into closer harmony. Each trial of voice, each fresh discovery of discord, almost imperceptibly induces the less perfect to modify his or her vocal utterance so as to approximate to the more perfect. And after many trials and many approximations, the result is at last achieved. There comes a day at last, when, while the wonted Marriage Chorus goes forth from universal Lineland, the three far-off Lovers suddenly find themselves in exact harmony, and, before they are aware, the wedded Triplet is rapt vocally into a duplicate embrace; and Nature rejoices over one more marriage and over three more births."

§ 2.—How I vainly tried to explain the nature

of Flatland.

Thinking that it was time to bring down the Monarch from his raptures to the level of common sense, I determined to endeavor to open up to him some glimpses of the truth, that is to say of the nature of things in Flatland. So I began thus: "How does your Royal Highness distinguish the shapes and positions of his subjects? I for my part noticed by the sense of sight, before I entered your Kingdom, that some of your people are Lines and others Points, and that some of the Lines are larger"

"You speak of an impossibility," interrupted the King; "you must have seen a vision; for to detect the difference between a Line and a Point by the sense of sight is, as everyone knows, in the nature of things, impossible; but it can be detected by the sense of hearing, and by the same means my shape can be exactly ascertained. Behold me—I am a Line, the longest in Lineland, over six inches of Space----"

"Of Length," I ventured to suggest.

"Fool," said he, "Space is Length. Interrupt me again, and I have done."

I apologized; but he continued scornfully, "Since you are impervious to argument, you shall hear with your ears how by means of my two voices I reveal my shape to my Wives, who are at this moment six thousand miles seventy yards two feet eight inches away, the one to the North, the other to the South. Listen, I call to them."

He chirruped, and then complacently continued: "My wives at this moment receiving the sound of one of my voices, closely followed by the other, and perceiving that the latter reaches them after an interval in which sound can traverse 6.457 inches, infer that one of my mouths is 6.457 inches further from them than the other, and accordingly know my shape to be 6.457 inches. But you will of course understand that my wives do not make this calculation every time they hear my two voices. They made it, once for all, before we were married. But they *could* make it at any time. And in the same way I can estimate the shape of any of my Male subjects by the sense of sound,"

"But how," said I," if a Man feigns a Woman's voice with one of his two voices, or so disguises his Southern voice that it cannot be recognized as the echo of the Northern? May not such deceptions cause great inconvenience? And have you no means of checking frauds of this kind by commanding your neighboring subjects to feel one another?" This of course was a very stupid question, for feeling could not have answered the purpose; but I asked with the view of irritating the Monarch, and I succeeded perfectly.

"What!" cried he in horror, "Explain your meaning." "Feel, touch, come into contact," I replied. "If you mean by *feeling*" said the King, "approaching so close as to leave no space between two individuals, know, Stranger, that this offence is punishable in my dominions by death. And the reason is obvious. The frail form of a Woman, being liable to be shattered by such an approximation, must be preserved by the State; but since Women cannot be distinguished by the sense of sight from Man, the Law ordains universally that neither Man nor Woman shall be approached so closely as to destroy the interval between the approximator and the approximated.

"And indeed what possible purpose would be served by this illegal and unnatural excess of approximation which you call *touching*, when all the ends of so brutal and coarse a process are attained at once more easily and more exactly by the sense of hearing. As to your suggested danger of deception, it is non-existent: for the Voice, being the essence of one's Being, cannot be thus changed at will. But come, suppose that I had the power of passing through solid things, so that I could penetrate my subjects, one after another, even to the number of a billion, verifying the size and distance of each by the sense of *feeling*: how much time and energy would be wasted in this clumsy and inaccurate method! Whereas now, in one moment of audition, I take as it were the census and statistics, local, corporal, mental, and spiritual, of every living being in Lineland. Hark, only hark!"

So saying he paused and listened, as if in an ecstasy, to a sound which seemed to me no better than a tiny chirping from an innumerable multitude of lilliputian grasshoppers.

"Truly," replied I, "your sense of hearing serves you in good stead, and fills up many of your deficiencies. But permit me to point out that your life in Lineland must be deplorably dull. To see nothing but a Point! Not even to be able to Contemplate a Straight Line! Nay, not even to know what a Straight Line is! To see, yet to be cut off from those Linear prospects which are vouchsafed to us in Flatland! Better surely to have no sense of sight at all than to see so little! I grant you I have not your discriminative faculty of hearing; for the concert of all Lineland which gives you such intense pleasure, is to me no better than a multitudinous twittering or chirping. But at least I can discern, by sight, a Line from a Point. And let me prove it. Just before I Came into your kingdom, I saw you dancing from left to right, and then from right to left, with seven Men and a Woman in your immediate proximity on the left, and eight Men and two Women on your right. Is not this correct? "

"It is correct," said the King, "so far as the numbers and sexes are concerned, though I know not what you mean by 'right' and 'left.' But I deny that you saw these things. For how could you see the Line, that is to say the inside, of any Man? But you must have heard these things, and then dreamed that you saw them. And let me ask what you mean by those words 'left' and 'right.' I suppose it is your way of saying Northward and Southward."

"Not so," replied I; "besides your motion of Northward and Southward, there is another motion which I call from right to left."

King. Exhibit to me, if you please, this motion from left to right.

I. Nay, that I cannot do, unless you could step out of your Line altogether.

King. Out of my Line? Do you mean out of the World? Out of Space?

I. Well, yes. Out of *your* World. Out of *your* Space. For your Space is not the true Space. True Space is a Plane; but your Space is only a Line.

King. If you cannot indicate this motion from left to right by yourself moving in it, then I beg you to describe it to me in words.

I. If you cannot tell your right side from my left, I fear that no words of mine can make my meaning clear to you. But surely you cannot be ignorant of so simple a distinction.

King. I do not in the least understand you.

I. Alas! How shall I make it clear? When you move straight on, does it not sometimes occur to you that you *could* move in some other way, turning your eye round so as to look in the direction towards which your side is now fronting? In other words, instead of always moving in the direction of one of your extremities, do you never feel a desire to move in the direction, so to speak, of your side?

King. Never. And what do you mean? How can a man's inside "front" in any direction? Or how can a man move in the direction of his inside?

I. Well then, since words cannot explain the matter, I will try deeds, and will move gradually out of Lineland in the direction which I desire to indicate to you.

At the word I began to move my body out of Lineland. As long as any part of me remained in his dominion and in his view, the King kept exclaiming, "I see you, I see you still; you are not moving." But when I had at last moved myself out of his Line, he cried in his shrillest voice, "She is vanished; she is dead." "I am not dead," replied I; "I am simply out of Lineland, that is to say, out of the Straight Line which you call Space, and in the true Space, where I can see things as they are. And at this moment I can see your Line, or side—or inside as you are pleased to call it; and I can also see the Men and Women on the North and South of you, whom I will now enumerate, describing their order, their size, and the interval between each,"

When I had done this at great length, I cried triumphantly, "Does this at last convince you?" And, with that, I once more entered Lineland, taking up the same position as before.

But the Monarch replied, "If you were a Man of sense——though, as you appear to have only one voice I have little doubt you are not a Man but a Woman—but, if you had a particle of sense, you would listen to reason. You ask me to believe that there is another Line besides that which my senses indicate, and another motion besides that of which I am daily conscious. I, in return, ask you to describe in words or indicate by motion that other Line of which you speak. Instead of moving, you merely exercise some magic art of vanishing and returning to sight; and instead of any lucid description of your new World, you simply tell me the numbers and sizes of some forty of my retinue, facts known to any child in my capital. Can anything be more irrational or audacious? Acknowledge your folly or depart from my dominions."

Furious at his perversity, and especially indignant that he professed to be ignorant of my Sex, I retorted in no measured terms, "Besotted Being! You think yourself the perfection of existence, while you are in reality the most imperfect and imbecile. You profess to see, whereas you can see nothing but a Point! You plume yourself on inferring the existence of a Straight Line; but I can see Straight Lines and infer the existence of Angles, Triangles, Squares, Pentagons, Hexagons, and even Circles. Why waste more words? Suffice it that I am the completion of your incomplete self. You are a Line, but I am a Line of Lines, called in my country a Square: and even I, infinitely superior though I am to you, am of little account among the great Nobles of Flatland, whence I have come to visit you, in the hope of enlightening your ignorance."

Hearing these words the King advanced towards me with a menacing cry as if to pierce me through the diagonal; and in that same moment there arose from myriads of his subjects a multitudinous war-cry, increasing in vehemence till at last methought it rivalled the roar of an army of a hundred thousand Isosceles, and the artillery of a thousand Pentagons. Spell-bound and motionless I could neither speak nor move to avert the impending destruction; and still the noise grew louder, and the King came closer, when I awoke to find the breakfast-bell recalling me to the realities of Flatland.

§ 3.—Concerning a Stranger from Spaceland.

From dreams I proceed to facts.

It was the last day of the 1999th year of our era. The pattering of the rain had long ago announced nightfall; and I was sitting in the company of my wife, musing on the events of the past and the prospects of the coming year, the coming century, the coming Millennium.

My four Sons and two orphan Grandchildren had retired to their several apartments; and my Wife alone remained with me to see the old Millennium out and the new one in.

I was rapt in thought, pondering in my mind some words that had casually issued from the mouth of my youngest Grandson, a most promising young Hexagon of unusual brilliancy and perfect angularity. His uncles and I had been giving him his usual practical lesson in Sight Recognition, turning ourselves upon our centres, now rapidly, now more slowly, and questioning him as to our positions; and his answers had been so satisfactory that I had been induced to reward him by giving him a few hints on Arithmetic, as applied to Geometry.

Taking nine Squares, each an inch every way, I had put them together so as to make one large Square, with a side of three inches, and I had hence proved to my little Grandson that—though it was impossible for us to see the inside of the Square—yet we might ascertain the number of square inches in a Square by simply squaring the number of inches in the side: "and thus," said I, "we know that 3^2, or 9, represents the number of square inches in a Square whose side is 3 inches long."

The little Hexagon meditated on this awhile and then said to me: "But you have been teaching me to raise numbers to the third power; I suppose 3^3 must mean something in Geometry; what does it mean?" "Nothing at all," replied I," not at least in Geometry; for Geometry has only Two Dimensions." And then I began to show the boy how a Point by moving through a length of three inches makes a Line of three inches, which may be represented by 3; and how a Line of three inches, moving parallel to itself through a length of three inches, makes a Square of three inches every way, which may be represented by 3^2.

Upon this, my Grandson, again returning to his former suggestion, took me up rather suddenly and exclaimed, "Well, then, if a Point by moving three inches, makes a Line of three inches represented by 3; and if a straight Line of three inches, moving parallel to itself, makes a Square of three inches every way, represented by 3^2; it must be that a Square of three inches every way, moving somehow parallel to itself (but I don't see how) must make a Something else (but I don't see what) of three inches every way—and this must be represented by 3^3."

"Go to bed," said I, a little ruffled by his interruption; "if you would talk less nonsense, you would remember more sense."

So my Grandson had disappeared in disgrace; and there I sat by my Wife's side, endeavoring to form a retrospect of the year 1999 and of the possibilities of the year 2000, but not quite able to shake off the thoughts suggested by the prattle of my bright little Hexagon. Only a few sands now remained in the half-hour glass. Rousing myself from my reverie I turned the glass Northward for the last time in the old Millennium; and in the act, I exclaimed aloud, "The boy is a fool."

Straightway I became conscious of a Presence in the room, and a chilling breath thrilled through my very being. "He is no such thing," cried my Wife, "and you are breaking the Commandments in thus dishonoring your own Grandson." But I took no notice of her. Looking round in every direction I could see nothing; yet still I *felt* a Presence, and shivered as the cold whisper came again. I started up. "What is the matter?" said my Wife, "there is no draught; what are you looking for? There is nothing." There was nothing; and I resumed my seat, again exclaiming, "The boy is a fool, I say; 33 can have no meaning in Geometry." At once there came a distinctly audible reply, "The boy is not a fool; and 33 has an obvious Geometrical meaning."

My Wife as well as myself heard the words, although she did not understand their meaning, and both of us sprang forward in the direction of the sound. What was our horror when we saw before us a Figure! At the first glance it appeared to be a Woman, seen sideways; but a moment's observation shewed me that the extremities passed into dimness too rapidly to represent one of the Female Sex;

and I should have thought it a Circle, only that it seemed to change its size in a manner impossible for a Circle or for any Regular Figure of which I had had experience.

But my Wife had not my experience, nor the coolness necessary to note these characteristics. With the usual hastiness and unreasoning jealousy of her Sex, she flew at once to the conclusion that a Woman had entered the house through some small aperture. "How comes this person here?" she exclaimed, "You promised me, my dear, that there should be no ventilators in our new house." "Nor are there any," said I; "but what makes you think that the stranger is a Woman? I see by my power of Sight Recognition." "Oh, I have no patience with your Sight Recognition," replied she, "'Feeling is believing' and 'A Straight Line to the touch is worth a Circle to the sight'"—two Proverbs, very common with the Frailer Sex in Flatland.

"Well," said I, for I was afraid of irritating her, "if it must be so, demand an introduction." Assuming her most gracious manner, my Wife advanced towards the Stranger, "Permit me, Madam, to feel and be felt by "then, suddenly recoiling," Oh! it is not a Woman, and there are no angles either, not a trace of one. Can it be that I have so misbehaved to a perfect Circle?"

"I am indeed, in a certain sense a Circle," replied the Voice, "and a more perfect Circle than any in Flatland; but to speak more accurately, I am many Circles in one." Then he added more mildly, "I have a message, dear Madam, to your husband, which I must not deliver in your presence; and, if you would suffer us to retire for a few minutes——" But my Wife would not listen to the proposal that our august Visitor should so incommode himself, and assuring the Circle that the hour for her own retirement had long passed, with many reiterated apologies for her recent indiscretion, she at last retreated to her apartment.

I glanced at the half-hour glass. The last sands had fallen. The second Millennium had begun.

§ 4.—How the Stranger vainly endeavored to reveal

to me in words the mysteries of Spaceland.

As soon as the sound of my Wife's retreating footsteps had died away, I began to approach the Stranger with the intention of taking a nearer view and of bidding him be seated: but his appearance struck me dumb and motionless with astonishment. Without the slightest symptoms of angularity he nevertheless varied every instant with gradations of size and brightness scarcely possible for any Figure within the scope of my experience. The thought flashed across me that I might have before me a burglar or cut-throat, some monstrous Irregular Isosceles, who, by feigning the voice of a Circle, had obtained admission somehow into the house, and was now preparing to stab me with his acute angle.

In a sitting-room, the absence of Fog (and the season happened to be remarkably dry), made it difficult for me to trust to Sight Recognition, especially at the short distance at which I was standing. Desperate with fear, I rushed forward with an unceremonious "You must permit me, Sir—" and felt him. My Wife was right. There was not the trace of an angle, not the slightest roughness or inequality: never in my life had I met with a more perfect Circle. He remained motionless while I walked round him, beginning from his eye and returning to it again. Circular he was throughout, a perfectly satisfactory Circle; there could not be a doubt of it. Then followed a dialogue, which I will endeavor to set down as near as I can recollect it, omitting only some of my profuse apologies—for I was covered with shame and humiliation that I, a Square, should have been guilty of the impertinence of feeling a Circle. It was commenced by the Stranger with some impatience at the lengthiness of my introductory process.

Stranger. Have you felt me enough by this time? Are you not introduced to me yet?

I. Most illustrious Sir, excuse my awkwardness, which arises not from ignorance of the usages of polite society, but from a little surprise and nervousness, consequent on this somewhat unexpected visit. And I beseech you to reveal my indiscretion to no one, and especially not to my Wife. But before your Lordship enters into further communications, would he deign to satisfy the curiosity of one who would gladly know whence his Visitor came?

Stranger. From Space, from Space, Sir: whence else?

I. Pardon me, my Lord, but is not your Lordship already in Space, your Lordship and his humble servant, even at this moment?

Stranger. Pooh! What do you know of Space? Define Space.

I. Space, my Lord, is height and breadth indefinitely prolonged.

Stranger. Exactly: you see you do not even know what Space is. You think it is of Two Dimensions only; but I have come to announce to you a Third— height, breadth, and length.

I. Your Lordship is pleased to be merry. We also speak of length and height, or breadth and thickness, thus denoting Two Dimensions by four names.

Stranger. But I mean not only three names, but Three Dimensions.

I. Would your Lordship indicate or explain to me in what direction is the Third Dimension, unknown to me?

Stranger. I came from it. It is up above and down below.

I. My Lord means seemingly that it is Northward and Southward.

Stranger. I mean nothing of the kind. I mean a direction in which you cannot look, because you have no eye in your side.

I. Pardon me, my Lord, a moment's inspection will convince your Lordship that I have a perfect luminary at the juncture of two of my sides.

Stranger. Yes: but in order to see into Space you ought to have an eye, not on your Perimeter, but on your side, that is, on what you would probably call your inside; but we in Spaceland should call it your side.

I. An eye in my inside! An eye in my stomach! Your Lordship jests.

Stranger. I am in no jesting humor. I tell you that I come from Space, or, since you will not understand what Space means, from the Land of Three Dimensions whence I but lately looked down upon your Plane which you call Space forsooth. From that position of advantage I discerned all that you speak of as *solid* (by which you mean "enclosed on four sides "), your houses, your churches, your very chests and safes, yes even your insides and stomachs, all lying open and exposed to my view.

I. Such assertions are easily made, my Lord.

Stranger. But not easily proved, you mean. But I mean to prove mine.

When I descended here, I saw your four Sons, the Pentagons, each in his apartment, and your two Grandsons the Hexagons; I saw your youngest Hexagon remain a while with you and then retire to his room, leaving you and your Wife alone. I saw your Isosceles servants, three in number, in the kitchen at supper, and the little Page in the scullery. Then I came here, and how do you think I came?

I. Through the roof, I suppose.

Stranger. Not so. Your roof, as you know very well, has been recently repaired, and has no aperture by which even a Woman could penetrate. I tell you I come from Space. Are you not convinced by what I have told you of your children and household.

I. Your Lordship must be aware that such facts touching the belongings of his humble servant might be easily ascertained by anyone in the neighborhood possessing your Lordship's ample means of obtaining information.

Stranger. How shall I convince him? Surely a plain statement of facts followed by ocular demonstration ought to suffice.—Now, Sir; listen to me.

You are living on a Plane. What you style Flatland is the vast level surface of what I may call a fluid, on, or in, the top of which you and your countrymen move about, without rising above it or falling below it.

I am not a plane Figure, but a Solid. You call me a Circle; but in reality I am not a Circle, but an infinite number of Circles, of size varying from a Point to a Circle of thirteen inches in diameter, one placed on the top of the other. When I cut through your plane as I am now doing, I make in your plane a section which you, very rightly, call a Circle. For even a Sphere—which is my proper name in my own country—if he manifest himself at all to an inhabitant of Flatland—must needs manifest himself as a Circle.

Do you not remember—for I, who see all things, discerned last night the phantasmal vision of Lineland written upon your brain—do you not remember, I say, how, when you entered the realm of Lineland, you were compelled to manifest yourself to the King not as a Square, but as a Line, because that Linear

Realm had not Dimensions enough to represent the whole of you, but only a slice or section of you? In precisely the same way, your country of Two Dimensions is not spacious enough to represent me, a being of Three, but can only exhibit a slice or section of me, which is what you call a Circle.

The diminished brightness of your eye indicates incredulity. But now prepare to receive proof positive of the truth of my assertions. You cannot indeed see more than one of my sections, or Circles, at a time; for you have no power to raise your eye out of the plane of Flatland; but you can at least see that, as I rise in Space, so my section becomes smaller. See now, I will rise; and the effect upon your eye will be that my Circle will become smaller and smaller till it dwindles to a point and finally vanishes.

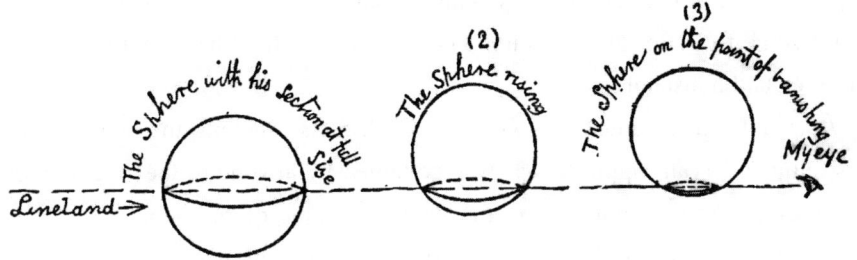

There was no "rising" that I could see; but he diminished and finally vanished. I winked once or twice to make sure that I was not dreaming. But it was no dream. For from the depths of nowhere came forth a hollow voice—close to my heart it seemed—" Am I quite gone? Are you convinced now? Well, now I will gradually return to Flatland, and you shall see my section become larger and larger."

Every reader in Spaceland will easily understand that my mysterious Guest was speaking the language of truth and even of simplicity. But to me, proficient though I was in Flatland Mathematics, it was by no means a simple matter. The rough diagram given above will make it clear to any Spaceland child that the Sphere, ascending in the three positions indicated there, must needs have manifested himself to me, or to any Flatlander, as a Circle, at first of full size, then small, and at last very small indeed, approaching to a Point. But to me, although I saw the facts before me, the causes were as dark as ever. All that I could comprehend was, that the Circle had made himself smaller and vanished, and that he had now reappeared and was rapidly making himself larger.

When he had regained his original size, he heaved a deep sigh; for he perceived by my silence that I had altogether failed to comprehend him. And indeed I was now inclining to the belief that he must be no Circle at all, but some extremely clever juggler; or else that the old wives' tales were true, and that after all there were such people as Enchanters and Magicians.

After a long pause he muttered to himself, "One resource alone remains, if I am not to resort to action. I must try the method of Analogy." Then followed a still longer silence, after which he continued our dialogue.

Sphere. Tell me, Mr. Mathematician; if a Point moves Northward, and leaves a luminous wake, what name would you give to the wake?

I. A straight Line.

Sphere. And a straight Line has how many extremities?

I. Two.

Sphere. Now conceive the Northward straight line moving parallel to itself, East and West, so that every point in it leaves behind it the wake of a straight Line. What name will you give to the Figure thereby formed? We will suppose that it moves through a distance equal to the original straight Line.—What name, I say?

I. A Square.

Sphere. And how many sides has a Square? And how many Angles?

I. Four sides and four angles.

Sphere. Now stretch your imagination a little, and conceive a Square in Flatland, moving parallel to itself upward.

I. What? Northward?

Sphere. No, not Northward; upward; out of Flatland altogether.

If it moved Northward, the Southern points in the Square would have to move through the positions previously occupied by the Northern points. But that is not my meaning.

I mean that every Point in you—for you are a Square and will serve the purpose of my illustration—every Point in you, that is to say in what you call your inside, is to pass upwards through Space in such a way that no Point shall pass through the position previously occupied by any other Point; but each Point shall describe a straight Line of its own. This is all in accordance with Analogy; surely it must be clear to you.

Restraining my impatience—for I was now under a strong temptation to rush blindly at my Visitor and to precipitate him into Space, or out of Flatland, anywhere, so that I could get rid of him—I replied:—

"And what may be the nature of the Figure which I am to shape out by this motion which you are pleased to denote by the word 'upward'? I presume it is describable in the language of Flatland."

Sphere. Oh, certainly. It is all plain and simple, and in strict accordance with Analogy—only, by the way, you must not speak of the result as being a Figure, but as a Solid. But I will describe it to you. Or rather not I, but Analogy.

We began with a single Point, which of course—being itself a Point —has only *one* terminal Point.

One Point produces a Line with *two* terminal Points.

One Line produces a Square with *four* terminal Points.

Now you can yourself give the answer to your own question: 1, 2, 4, are evidently in Geometrical Progression. What is the next number.

I. Eight.

Sphere. Exactly. The one Square produces a *Something-which-you-do-not-as-yet-know-a-name-for-but-which-we-call-a-Cube* with eight terminal Points. Now are you convinced?

I. And has this Creature sides, as well as angles or what you call "terminal Points?"

Sphere. Of course; and all according to Analogy. But, by the way, not what *you* call sides, but what *we* call sides. You would call them solids.

I. And how many solids or sides will appertain to this Being whom I am to generate by the motion of my inside in an "upward" direction, and whom you call a Cube?

Sphere. How can you ask? And you a mathematician! The side of anything is always, if I may so say, one Dimension behind the thing. Consequently, as there is no Dimension behind a Point, a Point has o sides; a Line, if I may so say, has 2 sides (for the Points of a Line may be called by courtesy, its sides); a Square has 4 sides; 0, 2, 4; what Progression do you call that?

I. Arithmetical.

Sphere. And what is the next number?

I. Six.

Sphere. Exactly. Then you see you have answered your own question. The Cube which you will generate will be bounded by six sides, that is to say, six of your insides. You see it all now, eh?

"Monster," I shrieked, "be thou juggler, enchanter, dream, or devil, no more will I endure thy mockeries. Either thou or I must perish." And saying these words I precipitated myself upon him.

§ 5.—How the Sphere, having in vain tried words,

resorted to deeds.

It was in vain. I brought my hardest right angle into violent collision with the Stranger, pressing on him with a force sufficient to have destroyed any ordinary Circle: but I could feel him slowly and unarrestably slipping from my contact; not edging to the right nor to the left, but moving somehow out of the world and vanishing to nothing. Soon there was a blank. But I still heard the Intruder's voice.

Sphere. Why will- you refuse to listen to reason? I had hoped to find in you— as being a man of sense and an accomplished mathematician—a fit apostle for the Gospel of the Three Dimensions, which I am allowed to preach once only in a thousand years: but now I know not how to convince you. Stay, I have it. Deeds, and not words, shall proclaim the truth. Listen, my friend.

I have told you I can see from my position in Space the inside of all things that you consider closed. For example, I see in yonder cupboard near which you are standing, several of what you call boxes (but like everything else in Flatland, they have no tops nor bottoms) full of money; I see also two tablets of accounts. I am about to descend into that cupboard and to bring you one of those tablets. I saw you lock the cupboard half an hour ago, and I know you have the key in your possession. But I descend from Space; the doors, you see, remain unmoved. Now I am in the cupboard and am taking the tablet. Now I have it. Now I ascend with it.

I rushed to the closet and dashed the door open. One of the tablets was gone. With a mocking laugh, the Stranger appeared in the other corner of the room, and at the same time the tablet appeared upon the floor. I took it up. There could be no doubt—it was the missing tablet.

I groaned with horror, doubting whether I was not out of my senses; but the Stranger continued: "Surely you must now see that my explanation, and no other,

suits the phenomena; What you call Solid things are really superficial; what you
call Space is really nothing but a great Plane. I am in Space, and look down upon
the insides of the things of which you only see the outsides. You could leave
this Plane yourself, if you could but summon up the necessary volition. A slight
upward or downward motion would enable you to see all that I can see.

"The higher I mount, and the further I go from your Plane, the more I can see,
though of course I see it on a smaller scale. For example, I am ascending; now
I can see your neighbor the Hexagon and his family in their several apartments;
now I see the inside of the Theatre, ten doors off, from which the audience is
only just departing; and on the other side a Circle in his study, sitting at his
books. Now I shall come back to you. And, as a crowning proof, what do you
say to my giving you a touch, just the least touch, in your stomach? It will not
seriously injure you, and the slight pain you may suffer cannot be compared with
the mental benefit you will receive."

Before I could utter a word of remonstrance, I felt a shooting pain in my
inside, and a demoniacal laugh seemed to issue from within me. A moment
afterwards the sharp agony had ceased, leaving nothing but a dull ache behind,
and the Stranger began to reappear, saying, as he gradually increased in size,
"There, I have not hurt you much, have I? If you are not convinced now, I don't
know what will convince you. What say you?"

My resolution was taken. It seemed intolerable that I should endure existence
subject to the arbitrary visitations of a Magician who could thus play tricks with
one's very stomach. If only I could in any way manage to pin him against the
wall till help came!

Once more I dashed my hardest angle against him, at the same time alarming
the whole household by my cries for aid. I believe, at the moment of my onset,
the Stranger had sunk below our Plane, and really found difficulty in rising. In
any case he remained motionless, while I, hearing, as I thought, the sound of
some help approaching, pressed against him with redoubled vigor, and continued
to shout for assistance.

A convulsive shudder ran through the Sphere. "This must not be," I thought
I heard him say; "either he must listen to reason, or I must have recourse to the
last resource of civilization." Then, addressing me in a louder tone, he hurriedly

exclaimed, "Listen: no stranger must witness what you have witnessed. Send your Wife back at once, before she enters the apartment. The Gospel of Three Dimensions must not be thus frustrated. Not thus must the fruits of one thousand years of waiting be thrown away. I hear her coming. Back! back! Away from me, or you must go with me—whither you know not—into the Land of Three Dimensions!"

"Fool! Madman! Irregular!" I exclaimed; "never will I release thee; thou shalt pay the penalty of thine impostures."

"Ha! Is it come to this?" thundered the Stranger: "then meet your fate: out of your Plane you go. Once, twice, thrice! 'Tis done!"

§ 6.—How I came to Space land, and what I saw there.

An unspeakable horror seized me. There was a darkness; then a dizzy, sickening sensation of sight that was not like seeing; I saw a Line that was no Line; Space that was not Space; I was myself, and not myself. When I could find voice, I shrieked aloud in agony, "Either this is madness or it is Hell." "It is neither," calmly replied the voice of the Sphere, "it is Knowledge; it is Three Dimensions: open your eye once again and try to look steadily."

I looked, and, behold, a new world! There stood before me, visibly incorporate, all that I had before inferred, conjectured, dreamed, of perfect Circular beauty. What seemed the centre of the Stranger's form lay open to my view: yet I could see no heart, nor lungs, nor arteries, only a beautiful harmonious Something—for which I had no words; but you, my Readers in Spaceland, would call it the surface of the Sphere.

Prostrating myself mentally before my Guide, I cried, "How is it, O divine ideal of consummate loveliness and wisdom, that I see thy inside, and yet cannot discern thy heart, thy lungs, thy arteries, thy liver?" "What you think you see, you see not," he replied; "it is not given to you, nor to any other Being, to behold my internal parts. I am of a different order of Beings from those in Flatland. Were I a Circle, you could discern my intestines, but I am a Being composed, as I told you before, of many Circles, the Many in the One, called in this country a Sphere. And, just as the outside of a Cube is a Square, so the outside of a Sphere presents the appearance of a Circle."

Bewildered though I was by my Teacher's enigmatic utterance, I no longer chafed against it, but worshipped him in silent adoration. He continued, with more mildness in his voice: "Distress not yourself if you cannot at first understand the deeper mysteries of Spaceland. By degrees they will dawn upon you. Let us begin by casting back a glance at the region whence you came. Return with me a while to the plains of Flatland, and I will show you that which you have so often reasoned and thought about, but never seen with the sense of sight—a visible angle." "Impossible!" I cried; but, the Sphere leading the way, I followed as if in a dream, till once more his voice arrested me: "Look yonder, and behold your own Pentagonal house and all its inmates."

I looked below, and saw with my physical eye all that domestic individuality which I had hitherto merely inferred with the understanding. And how poor and shadowy was the inferred conjecture in comparison with the reality which I now beheld! My four Sons calmly asleep in the North-Western rooms, my two orphan Grandsons to the South; the Servants, the Butler, my Daughter, all in their several apartments. Only my affectionate Wife, alarmed by my continued absence, had quitted her room and was roving up and down in the Hall, anxiously awaiting my return. Also the Page, aroused by my cries, had left his room, and under pretext of ascertaining whether, I had fallen somewhere in a faint, was prying into the cabinet in my study. All this I could now see, not merely infer; and as we came nearer and nearer, I could discern even the contents of my cabinet, and the two chests of gold, and the tablets of which the Sphere had made mention.

Touched by my Wife's distress, I would have sprung downward to reassure her, but I found myself incapable of motion. "Trouble not yourself about your Wife," said my Guide; "she will not be long left in anxiety; meantime, let us take a survey of Flatland."

Once more I felt myself rising through space. It was even as the Sphere had said. The further we receded from the object we beheld, the larger became

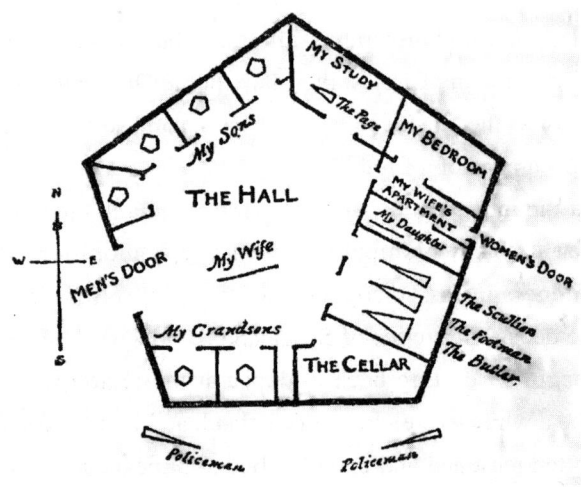

the field of vision. My native city, with the interior of every house and every creature therein, lay open to my view in miniature. We mounted higher, and lo, the secrets of the earth, the depths of mines and inmost caverns of the hills, were bared before me.

Awestruck at the sight of the mysteries of the earth, thus unveiled before my unworthy eye, I said to my Companion, "Behold, I am become as a God. For the wise men in our country say that to see all things, or as they express it, *omnividence*, is the attribute of God alone." There was something of scorn in the voice of my Teacher as he made answer: "Is it so indeed? Then the very pickpockets and cut-throats of my country are to be worshipped by your wise men as being Gods: for there is not one of them that does not see as much as you see now. But trust me, your wise men are wrong."

I. Then is omnividence the attribute of others beside Gods?

Sphere. I do not know. But, if a pick-pocket or a cut-throat -of our country can see everything that is in your country, surely that is no reason why the pick-pocket or cut-throat should be accepted by you as a God. This omnividence, as you call it—it is not a common word in Spaceland—does it make you more just, more merciful, less selfish, more loving? Not in the least. Then how does it make you more divine?

I. "More merciful, more loving!" But these are the qualities of women! And we know that a Circle is a higher Being than a Straight Line, in so far as knowledge and wisdom are more to be esteemed than mere affection.

Sphere. It is not for me to classify human faculties according to merit. Yet many of the best and wisest in Spaceland think more of the affections than of the understanding, more of your despised Straight Lines than of your belauded Circles. But enough of this. Look yonder. Do you know that building?

I looked, and afar off I saw an immense Polygonal structure, in which I recognized the General Assembly Hall of the States of Flatland, surrounded by dense lines of Pentagonal buildings at right angles to each other, which I knew to be streets; and I perceived that I was approaching the great Metropolis.

"Here we descend," said my Guide. It was now morning, the first hour of the first day of the two thousandth year of our era. Acting, as was their wont, in strict accordance with precedent, the highest Circles of the realm were meeting in solemn conclave, as they had met on the first hour of the first day of the year 1000, and also on the first hour of the first day of the year 0.

The minutes of the previous meetings were now read by one whom I at once recognized as my brother, a perfectly Symmetrical Square, and the Chief Clerk of the High Council. It was found recorded on each occasion that: "Whereas the States had been troubled by divers ill-intentioned persons pretending to have received revelations from another World, and professing to produce demonstrations whereby they had instigated to frenzy both themselves and others, it had been for this cause unanimously resolved by the Grand Council that on the first day of each millenary, special injunctions be sent to the Prefects in the several districts of Flatland, to make strict search for such misguided persons, and without formality of mathematical examination, to destroy all such as were Isosceles of any degree, to scourge and imprison any regular Triangle, to cause any Square or Pentagon to be sent to the district Asylum, and to arrest anyone of higher rank, sending him straightway to the Capital to be examined and judged by the Council."

"You hear your fate," said the Sphere to me, while the Council was passing for the third time the formal resolution. "Death or imprisonment awaits the Apostle of the Gospel of Three Dimensions." "Not so," replied I, "the matter is now so clear to me, the nature of real space so palpable, that methinks I could make a child understand it. Permit me but to descend at this moment and enlighten them." "Not yet," said my Guide, "the time will come for that. Meantime I must perform my mission. Stay thou there in thy place." Saying these words, he leaped with great dexterity into the sea (if I may so call it) of Flatland, right in the midst of the ring of Counsellors. "I come," cried he, "to proclaim that there is a land of Three Dimensions."

I could see many of the younger Counsellors start back in manifest horror, as the Sphere's circular section widened before them. But on a sign from the presiding Circle,—who showed not the slightest alarm or surprise—six Isosceles of a low type from six different quarters rushed upon the Sphere. "We have him," they cried; "No; Yes; We have him still! He's going! He's gone!"

"My Lords," said the President to the Junior Circles of the Council, "there is not the slightest need for surprise; the secret archives, to which I alone have access, tell me that a similar occurrence happened on the last two millennial commencements. You will, of course, say nothing of these trifles outside the Cabinet."

Raising his voice, he now summoned the guard. "Arrest the policemen; gag them. You know your duty." After he had consigned to their fate the wretched policemen—ill-fated and unwilling witnesses of a State-secret which they were not to be permitted to reveal—he again addressed the Counsellors. "My Lords, the business of the Council being concluded, I have only to wish you a happy New Year." Before departing, he expressed, at some length, to the Clerk, my excellent but most unfortunate brother, his sincere regret that, in accordance with precedent and for the sake of secrecy, he must condemn him to perpetual imprisonment, but added his satisfaction that, unless some mention were made by him of that day's incident, his life would be spared.

§ 7.—How, though the Sphere showed me other mysteries of Spaceland, I still desired more; and what came of it.

When I saw my poor brother led away to imprisonment, I attempted to leap down into the Council Chamber, desiring to intercede on his behalf, or at least bid him farewell. But I found that I had no motion of my own. I absolutely depended on the volition of my Guide, who said in gloomy tones, "Heed not thy brother; haply thou shalt have ample time hereafter to condole with him. Follow me."

Once more we ascended into space. "Hitherto," said the Sphere, "I have shown you naught save Plane Figures and their interiors. Now I must introduce you to Solids, and reveal to you the plan upon which they are constructed. Behold this multitude of moveable square cards. See, I put one on another, not, as you supposed, Northward of the other, but *on* the other. Now a second, now a third. See, I am building up a Solid by a multitude of Squares parallel to one another. Now the Solid is complete, being as high as it is long and broad, and we call it a Cube."

"Pardon me, my Lord," replied I; "but to my eye the appearance is as of an Irregular Figure whose inside is laid open to the view; in other words, methinks I see no Solid, but a Plane such as we infer in Flatland; only of an Irregularity which betokens some monstrous criminal, so that the very sight of it is painful to my eyes."

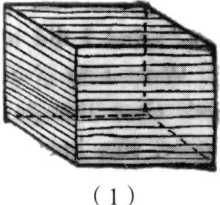

(1)

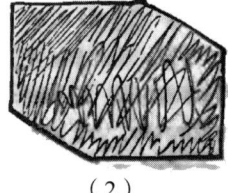

(2)

"True," said the Sphere; "it appears to you a Plane, because you are not accustomed to light and shade and perspective; just as in Flatland a Hexagon would appear a Straight Line to one who has not the Art of Sight Recognition. But in reality it is a Solid, as you shall learn by the sense of Feeling."

He then introduced me to the Cube, and I found that this marvelous Being was indeed no Plane, but a Solid; and that he was endowed with six plane sides and eight terminal points called solid angles; and I remembered the saying of the Sphere that just such a Creature as this would be formed by a Square moving, in Space, parallel to himself: and I rejoiced to think that so insignificant a Creature as I could in some sense be called the Progenitor of so illustrious an offspring.

But still I could not fully understand the meaning of what my Teacher had told me concerning "light" and "shade" and "perspective"; and I did not hesitate to put my difficulties before him.

Were I to give the Sphere's explanation of these matters, succinct and clear though it was, it would be tedious to an inhabitant of Space, who knows these things already. Suffice it, that by his lucid statements, and by changing the position of objects and lights, and by allowing me to feel the several objects and even his own sacred Person, he at last made all things clear to me, so that I could now readily distinguish between a Circle and a Sphere, a Plane Figure and a Solid.

This was the Climax, the Paradise, of my strange eventful History. Henceforth I have to relate the story of my miserable Fall:—most miserable, yet surely most undeserved! For why should the thirst for knowledge be aroused, only to be disappointed and punished! My volition shrinks from the painful task of recalling my humiliation; yet, like a second Prometheus, I will endure this and worse, if by any means I may arouse in the interiors of Plane and Solid Humanity a spirit of rebellion against the Conceit which would limit our Dimensions to Two or Three or any number short of Infinity. Away then with all personal considerations! Let me continue to the end, as I began, without further digressions or anticipations, pursuing the plain path of dispassionate History. The exact facts, the exact words,— and they are burnt in upon my brain,—shall be set down without alteration of an iota; and let my Readers judge between me and Destiny.

The Sphere would willingly have continued his lessons by indoctrinating me in the conformation of all regular Solids, Cylinders, Cones, Pyramids, Pentahedrons, Hexahedrons, Dodecahedrons and Spheres: but I ventured to interrupt him. Not that I was wearied of knowledge. On the contrary, I thirsted for yet deeper and fuller draughts than he was offering to me.

"Pardon me," said I, "O Thou Whom I must no longer address as the Perfection of all Beauty; but let me beg thee to vouchsafe thy servant a sight of thine interior."

Sphere. "My what?"

I. "Thine interior: thy stomach, thy intestines."

Sphere. "Whence this ill-timed impertinent request? And what mean you by saying that I am no longer the Perfection of all Beauty?"

I. My Lord, your own wisdom has taught me to aspire to One even more great, more beautiful, and more closely approximate to Perfection than yourself. As you yourself, superior to all Flatland forms, combine many Circles in One, so doubtless there is One above you who combines many Spheres in One Supreme Existence, surpassing even the Solids of Spaceland. And even as we, who are now in Space, look down on Flatland and see the insides of all things, so of a certainty there is yet above us some higher, purer region, whither thou dost surely purpose to lead me—O Thou Whom I shall always call, everywhere and in all Dimensions, my Priest, Philosopher, and Friend—some yet more spacious Space, some more dimensionable Dimensionality, from the vantage-ground of which we shall look down together upon the revealed insides of Solid things, and where thine own intestines, and those of thy kindred Spheres, will lie exposed to the view of the poor wandering exile from Flatland, to whom so much has already been vouchsafed.

Sphere. Pooh! Stuff! Enough of this trifling! The time is short, and much remains to be done before you are fit to proclaim the Gospel of Three Dimensions to your blind benighted countrymen in Flatland.

I. Nay, gracious Teacher, deny me not what I know it is in thy power to perform. Grant me but one glimpse of thine interior, and I am satisfied for ever, remaining henceforth thy docile pupil, thy unemancipable slave, ready to receive all thy teachings and to feed upon the words that fall from thy lips.

Sphere. Well, then, to content and silence you, let me say at once, I would show you what you wish if I could; but I cannot. Would you have me turn my stomach inside out to oblige you?

I. But my Lord has shown me the intestines of all my countrymen in the Land of Two Dimensions by taking me with him into the Land of Three. What therefore more easy than now to take his servant on a second journey into the blessed region of the Fourth Dimension, where I shall look down with him once more upon this land of Three Dimensions, and see the inside of every three-dimensioned house, the secrets of the solid earth, the treasures of the mines in Spaceland, and the intestines of every solid living creature, even of the noble and adorable Spheres.

Sphere. But where is this land of Four Dimensions?

I. I know not: but doubtless my Teacher knows.

Sphere. Not I. There is no such land. The very idea of it is utterly inconceivable.

I. Your Lordship tempts his servant to see whether he remembers the revelations imparted to him. Trifle not with me, my Lord; I crave, I thirst, for more knowledge. Doubtless we cannot see that other higher Spaceland now, because we have no eye in our stomachs. But, just as there *was* the realm of Flatland, though that poor puny Lineland Monarch could neither turn to left nor right to discern it, and just as there *was* close at hand, and touching my frame, the land of Three Dimensions, though I, blind senseless wretch, had no power to touch it, no eye in my interior to discern it, so of a surety there is a Fourth Dimension, which my Lord perceives with the inner eye of thought. And that it must exist my Lord himself has taught me. Or can he have forgotten what he himself imparted to his servant?

In One Dimension, did not a moving Point produce a Line with *two* terminal points?

In Two Dimensions, did not a moving Line produce a Square with *four* terminal points?

In Three Dimensions, did not a moving Square produce—did not this eye of mine behold it—that blessed Being, a Cube, with *eight* terminal points?

And in Four Dimensions shall not a moving Cube—alas, for Analogy, and alas for the Progress of Truth, if it be not so—shall not, I say, the motion of a divine Cube result in a still more divine Organization with *sixteen* terminal points?

Behold the infallible confirmation of the Series, 2, 4, 8, 16: is not this a Geometrical Progression? Is not this—if I might quote my Lord's own words— "strictly according to Analogy "?

Again, was I not taught by my Lord that as in a Line there are *two* bounding Points, and in a Square there are *four* bounding Lines, so in a Cube there must be *six* bounding Squares? Behold once more the confirming Series, 2, 4, 6: is not this an Arithmetical Progression? And consequently does it not of necessity follow that the more divine offspring of the divine Cube in the Land of Four Dimensions, must have 8 bounding Cubes: and is not this also, as my Lord has taught me to believe, "strictly according to Analogy"?

O, my Lord, my Lord, behold, I cast myself in faith upon conjecture, not knowing the facts; and I appeal to your Lordship to confirm or deny my logical anticipations. If I am wrong, I yield, and will no longer demand a Fourth Dimension; but, if I am right, my Lord will listen to reason.

I ask therefore, is it, or is it not, the fact, that ere now your countrymen also have witnessed the descent of Beings of a higher order than their own, entering closed rooms, even as your Lordship entered mine, without the opening of doors or windows, and appearing and vanishing at will? On the reply to this question I am ready to stake everything. Deny it, and I am henceforth silent. Only vouchsafe an answer.

Sphere (*after a pause*). It is reported so. But men are divided in opinion as to the facts. And even granting the facts, they explain them in different ways. And in any case, however great may be the number of different explanations, no one has adopted or suggested the theory of a Fourth Dimension. Therefore, pray have done with this trifling, and let us return to business.

I. I was certain of it. I was certain that my anticipations would be fulfilled. And now have patience with me and answer me yet one more question, best of Teachers! Those who have thus appeared—no one knows whence—and have returned—no one knows whither—have they also contracted their sections and vanished somehow into that more Spacious Space, whither I now entreat you to conduct me?

Sphere (*moodily*). They have vanished, certainly—if they ever appeared. But most people say that these visions arose from the thought— you will not understand me—from the brain; from the perturbed angularity of the Seer.

I. Say they so? Oh, believe them not. Or if it indeed be so, that this other Space is really Thoughtland, then take me to that blessed Region where I in Thought shall see the insides of all solid things. There, before my ravished eye, a Cube, moving in some altogether new direction, but strictly according to Analogy, so as to make every particle of his interior pass through a new kind of Space with a wake of its own— shall create a still more perfect perfection than himself, with sixteen terminal Extra-solid angles, and Eight solid Cubes for his Perimeter. And once there, shall we stay our upward course? In that blessed region of Four Dimensions, shall we linger on the threshold of the Fifth, and not enter therein? Ah, no! Let us rather resolve that our ambition shall soar with our corporal ascent. Then, yielding to our intellectual onset, the gates of the Sixth Dimension shall fly open; after that a Seventh, and then an Eighth

How long I should have continued I know not. In vain did the Sphere, in his voice of thunder, reiterate his commands of silence, and threaten me with the direst penalties if I persisted. Nothing could stem the flood of my ecstatic aspirations. Perhaps I was to blame; but indeed I was intoxicated with the recent draughts of Truth to which he himself had introduced me. However, the end was not long in coming. My words were cut short by a crash outside, and a simultaneous crash inside me, which impelled me through Space with a velocity that precluded speech. Down! Down! Down! I was rapidly descending; and I knew that return to Flatland was my doom. One glimpse, one last and never-to-be-forgotten glimpse I had of that dull level wilderness—which was now to become my Universe again—spread out before my eye. Then a darkness. Then a final, all-consummating thunder-peal; and, when I came to myself, I was once more a common creeping Square, in my Study at home, listening to the Peace-Cry of my approaching Wife.

§ 8.—How the Sphere encouraged me in a Vision.

Although I had less than a minute for reflection, I felt, by a kind of instinct, that I must conceal my experiences from my Wife. Not that I apprehended, at the moment, any danger from her divulging my secret, but I know that to any Woman in Flatland the narrative of my adventures must needs be unintelligible. So I endeavored to reassure her by some story, invented for the occasion, that I had accidentally fallen through the trap-door of the cellar, and had there lain stunned.

The Southward attraction in our country is so slight that even to a Woman my tale necessarily appeared extraordinary and well-nigh incredible; but my Wife, whose good sense far exceeds that of the average of her Sex, and who perceived that I was unusually excited, did not argue with me on the subject, but insisted that I was ill and required repose. I was glad of an excuse for retiring to my chamber to think quietly over what had happened. When I was at last by myself, a drowsy sensation fell on me; but before my eyes closed I endeavored to reproduce the Third Dimension, and especially the process by which a Cube is constructed through the motion of a Square. It was not so clear as I could have wished; but I remembered that it must be "Upward, and yet not Northward," and I determined steadfastly to retain these words as the clue which, if firmly grasped, could not fail to guide me to the solution. So mechanically repeating, like a charm, the words, "Upward yet not Northward," I fell into a sound refreshing sleep.

During my slumber I had a dream. I thought I was once more by the side of the Sphere, whose lustrous hue betokened that he had exchanged his wrath against me for perfect placability. We were moving together towards a bright but infinitesimally small Point, to which my Master directed my attention. As we approached, methought there issued from it a slight humming noise as from one of your Spaceland blue-bottles, only less resonant by far, so slight indeed that even in the perfect stillness of the Vacuum through which we soared, the sound reached not our ears till we checked our flight at a distance from it of something under twenty human diagonals.

"Look yonder," said my Guide, "in Flatland thou hast lived; of Lineland thou hast received a vision; thou hast soared with me to the heights of Spaceland; now, in order to complete the range of thy experience, I conduct thee downward to the lowest depth of existence, even to the realm of Pointland, the Abyss of No Dimensions.

"Behold yon miserable creature. That Point is a Being like ourselves, but confined to the non-dimensional Gulf. He is himself his own World, his own Universe; of any other than himself he can form no conception; he knows not Length, nor Breadth, nor Height, for he has had no experience of them; he has no cognizance even of the number Two; nor has he a thought of Plurality; for he is himself his One and All, being really Nothing. Yet mark his perfect self-contentment, and hence learn this lesson, that to be self-contented is to be vile and ignorant, and that to aspire is better than to be blindly and impotently happy. Now listen."

He ceased; and there arose from the little buzzing creature a tiny, low, monotonous, but distinct tinkling, as from one of your Spaceland phonographs, from which I caught these words, "Infinite beatitude of existence! It is; and there is none else beside It."

"What," said I, "does the puny creature mean by 'it'?" "He means himself," said the Sphere: "have you not noticed before now, that babies and babyish people who cannot distinguish themselves from the world, speak of themselves in the Third Person? But hush!"

"It fills all Space," continued the little soliloquizing Creature, "and what It fills, It is. What It thinks, that It utters; and what It utters, that It hears; and It itself is Thinker, Utterer, Hearer, Thought, Word, Audition; it is the One, and yet the All in All. Ah, the happiness, ah, the happiness of Being! "

"Can you not startle the little thing out of its complacency?" said I. "Tell it what it really is, as you told me; reveal to it the narrow limitations of Pointland, and lead it up to something higher." "That is no easy task," said my Master; "try you."

Hereon, raising my voice to the uttermost, I addressed the Point as follows:

"Silence, silence, contemptible Creature. You call yourself the All in All, but you are the Nothing: your so-called Universe is a mere speck in a Line, and a Line is a mere shadow as compared with—" "Hush, hush, you have said enough," interrupted the Sphere, "now listen, and mark the effect of your harangue on the King of Pointland."

The lustre of the Monarch, who beamed more brightly than ever upon hearing my words, showed clearly that he retained his complacency; and I had hardly ceased when he took up his strain again. "Ah, the joy, ah, the joy of Thought! What can It not achieve by thinking! Its own Thought coming to Itself, suggestive of Its disparagement, thereby to enhance Its happiness! Sweet rebellion stirred up to result in triumph! Ah, the divine creative power of the All in One! Ah, the joy, the joy of Being! "

"You see," said my Teacher, "how little your words have done. So far as the Monarch understands them at all, he accepts them as his own—for he cannot conceive of any other except himself—and plumes himself upon the variety of 'Its Thought' as an instance of creative Power. Let us leave this God of Pointland to the ignorant fruitiòn of his omnipresence and omniscience: nothing that you or I can do can rescue him from his self-satisfaction."

After this, as we floated gently back to Flatland, I could hear the mild voice of my Companion pointing the moral of my vision, and stimulating me to aspire, and to teach others to aspire. He had been angered at first—he confessed—by my ambition to soar to Dimensions above the Third; but, since then, he had received fresh insight, and he was not too proud to acknowledge his error to a Pupil. Then he proceeded to initiate me into mysteries yet higher than those I had witnessed, showing me how to construct Extra-Solids by the motion of Solids, and Double Extra-Solids by the motion of Extra-Solids, and all "strictly according to Analogy," all by methods so simple, so easy, as to be patent even to the Female Sex.

§ 9.—How I tried to teach the theory of Three Dimensions to my Grandson, and with what success.

I awoke rejoicing, and began to reflect on the glorious career before me. I would go forth, methought, at once, and evangelize the whole of Flatland. Even to Women and Soldiers should the Gospel of Three Dimensions be proclaimed. I would begin with my Wife.

Just as I had decided on the plan of my operations, I heard the sound of many voices in the street commanding silence. Then followed a louder voice. It was a herald's proclamation. Listening attentively, I recognized the words of the Resolution of the Council, enjoining the arrest, imprisonment, or execution of any one who should pervert the minds of the people by delusions, and by professing to have received revelations from another World.

I reflected. This danger was not to be trifled with. It would be better to avoid it by omitting all mention of my Revelation, and by proceeding on the path of Demonstration—which after all, seemed so simple and so conclusive that nothing would be lost by discarding the former means. "Upward, not Northward "—was the clue to the whole proof. It had seemed to me fairly clear before I fell asleep; and when I first awoke, fresh from my dream, it had appeared as patent as Arithmetic; but somehow it did not seem to me quite so obvious now. Though my Wife entered the room opportunely just at that moment, I decided, after we had interchanged a few words of commonplace conversation, not to begin with her.

My Pentagonal Sons were men of character and standing, and physicians of no mean reputation, but not great in mathematics, and, in that respect, unfit for my purpose. But it occurred to me that a young and docile Hexagon, with a mathematical turn, would be a most suitable pupil. Why therefore not make my first experiment with my little precocious Grandson, whose casual remarks on the meaning of 33 had met with the approval of the Sphere? Discussing the matter with him, a mere boy, I should be in perfect safety; for he would know nothing of the Proclamation of the Council; whereas I could not feel sure that my Sons—so greatly did their patriotism and reverence for the Circles predominate over mere blind affection—might not feel compelled to hand me over to the Prefect, if they found me seriously maintaining the seditious heresy of the Third Dimension.

But the first thing to be done was to satisfy in some way the curiosity of my Wife, who naturally wished to know something of the reasons for which the Circle had desired that mysterious interview, and of the means by which he had entered our house. Without entering into the details of the elaborate account I gave her,—an account, I fear, not quite so consistent with truth as my Readers in Spaceland might desire, — I must be content with saying that I succeeded at last in persuading her to return quietly to her household duties without eliciting from me any reference to the World of Three Dimensions. This done, I immediately sent for my Grandson; for, to confess the truth, I felt that all that I had seen and heard was in some strange way slipping away from me, like the image of a half-grasped, tantalizing dream, and I longed to essay my skill in making a first disciple.

When my Grandson entered the room I carefully secured the door. Then, sitting down by his side and taking our mathematical tablets—or, as you would call them, Lines—I told him we would resume the lesson of yesterday. I taught him once more how a Point by motion in One Dimension produces a Line, and how a straight Line in Two Dimensions produces a Square. After this, forcing a laugh, I said, "And now, you scamp, you wanted to make me believe that a Square may in the same way by motion 'Upward, not Northward,' produce another figure, a sort of extra Square in Three Dimensions. Say that again, you young rascal."

At this moment we heard once more the herald's "O yes! O yes!" outside in the street proclaiming the Resolution of the Council. Young though he was, my Grandson—who was unusually intelligent for his age, and bred up in perfect reverence for the authority of the Circles— took in the situation with an acuteness for which I was quite unprepared. He remained silent till the last words of the Proclamation had died away, and then, bursting into tears, "Dear

Grandpapa," he said, "that was only my fun, and of course I meant nothing at all by it; and we did not know anything then about the new Law; and I don't think I said anything about the Third Dimension; and I am sure I did not say one word about 'Upward, not Northward,' for that would be such nonsense, you know. How could a thing move Upward, and not Northward? Upward, and not Northward! Even if I were a baby, I could not be so absurd as that. How silly it is! Ha! Ha! Ha! "

"Not at all silly," said I, losing my temper; "here for example, I take this Square," —and, at the word, I grasped a moveable Square, which was lying at hand— "and I move it, you see, not Northward but —yes, I move it Upward— that is to say, not Northward, but I move it somewhere—not exactly like this, but somehow—" Here I brought my sentence to an inane conclusion, shaking the Square about in a purposeless manner, much to the amusement of my Grandson, who burst out laughing louder than ever, and declared that I was not teaching him, but joking with him; and so saying he unlocked the door and ran out of the room. Thus ended my first attempt to convert a pupil to the Gospel of Three Dimensions.

§ 10.—How I then tried to diffuse the Theory of Three Dimensions by other means, and of the result.

My failure with my Grandson did not encourage me to communicate my secret to others of my household; yet neither was I led by it to despair of success. Only I saw that I must not wholly rely on the catch-phrase "Upward, not Northward," but must rather endeavor to seek a demonstration by setting before the public a clear view of the whole subject; and for this purpose it seemed necessary to resort to writing.

So I devoted several months in privacy to the composition of a treatise on the mysteries of Three Dimensions. Only, with the view of evading the Law, if possible, I spoke not of a physical Dimension, but of a Thoughtland whence, in theory, a Figure could look down upon Flatland and see simultaneously the insides of all things, and where it was possible that there might be supposed to exist a Figure environed, as it were, with six Squares, and containing eight terminal Points. But in writing this book I found myself sadly hampered by the impossibility of drawing such diagrams as were necessary for my purpose; for of course, in our country of Flatland, there are no tablets but Lines, and no diagrams but Lines, all in one straight Line and only distinguishable by difference of size and brightness; so that, when I had finished my treatise (which I entitled "Through Flatland to Thoughtland") I could not feel certain that many would understand my meaning.

Meanwhile my life was under a cloud. All pleasures palled upon me; all sights tantalized and tempted me to outspoken treason, because I could not but compare what I saw in Two Dimensions with what it really was if seen in Three, and could hardly refrain from making my comparisons aloud. I neglected my clients and my own business to give myself to the contemplation of the mysteries which I had once beheld, yet which I could impart to no one, and found daily more difficult to reproduce even before my own mental vision.

One day, about eleven months after my return from Spaceland, I tried to see a Cube with my eye closed, but failed; and though I succeeded afterwards, I was not then quite certain (nor have I been ever afterwards) that I had exactly realized the original. This made me more, melancholy than before, and determined me to take some step; yet what, I knew not. I felt that I would have been willing to sacrifice my life for the Cause, if thereby I could have produced conviction. But if I could not convince my Grandson, how could I convince the highest and most developed Circles in the land?

And yet at times my spirit was too strong for me, and I gave vent to dangerous utterances. Already I was considered heterodox if not treasonable, and I was keenly alive to the dangers of my position; nevertheless I could not at times refrain from bursting out into suspicious or half-seditious utterances, even among the highest Polygonal and Circular society. When, for example, the question arose about the treatment of those lunatics who said that they had received the power of seeing the insides of things, I would quote the saying of an ancient Circle, who declared that prophets and inspired people are always considered by the majority to be mad; and I could not help occasionally dropping such expressions as "the eye that discerns the interiors of things," and "the all-seeing land:" once or twice I even let fall the forbidden terms "the Third and Fourth Dimensions." At last, to complete a series of minor indiscretions, at a meeting of our Local Speculative Society held at the palace of the Prefect himself,—some extremely silly person having read an elaborate paper exhibiting the precise reasons why Providence has limited the number of Dimensions to Two, and why the attribute of omnividence is assigned to the Supreme alone----I so far forgot myself as to give an exact account of the whole of my voyage with the Sphere into Space, and to the Assembly Hall in our Metropolis, and then to Space again, and of my return home, and of everything that I had seen and heard in fact or vision. At first, indeed, I pretended that I was describing the imaginary experiences of a fictitious person; but my enthusiasm soon forced me to throw off all disguise, and finally, in a fervent peroration, I exhorted all my hearers to divest themselves of prejudice and to become believers in the Third Dimension.

Need I say that I was at once arrested and taken before the Council?

Next morning, standing in the very place where but a very few months ago the Sphere had stood in my company, I was allowed to begin and to continue my narration unquestioned and uninterrupted. But from the first I foresaw my fate; for the President, noting that a guard of the better sort of Policemen was in attendance, of angularity little, if at all, under 55°, ordered them to be relieved before I began my defence, by an inferior class of 2° or 3°. I knew only too well what that meant. I was to be executed or imprisoned, and my story was to be kept secret from the world by the simultaneous destruction of the officials who had heard it; and, this being the case, the President desired to substitute the cheaper for the more expensive victims.

After I had concluded my defence, the President, perhaps perceiving that some of the junior Circles had been moved by my evident earnestness, asked me two questions:—

1. Whether I could indicate the direction which I meant when I used the words "Upward, not Northward "?

2. Whether I could by any diagrams or descriptions (other than the enumeration of imaginary sides and angles) indicate the Figure I was pleased to call a Cube?

I declared that I could say nothing more, and that I must commit myself to the Truth, whose cause would surely prevail in the end.

The President replied that he quite concurred in my sentiment, and that I could not do better. I must be sentenced to perpetual imprisonment; but if the Truth intended that I should emerge from prison and evangelize the world, the Truth might be trusted to bring that result to pass. Meanwhile I should be subjected to no discomfort that was not necessary to preclude escape, and, unless I forfeited the privilege by misconduct, I should be occasionally permitted to see my brother, who had preceded me to my prison.

Seven years have elapsed and I am still a prisoner, and—if I except the occasional visits of my brother—debarred from all companionship save that of my jailers. My brother is one of the best of Squares, just, sensible, cheerful, and not without fraternal affection; yet I must confess that my weekly interviews, at least in one respect, cause me the bitterest pain. He was present when the Sphere manifested himself in the Council Chamber; he saw the Sphere's changing sections; he heard the explanation of the phenomena then given to the Circles.

Since that time, scarcely a week has passed during seven whole years, without his hearing from me a repetition of the part I played in that manifestation, together with ample descriptions of all the phenomena in Spaceland, and the arguments for the existence of Solid things derivable from Analogy. Yet—I take shame to be forced to confess it—my brother has not yet grasped the nature of the Third Dimension, and frankly avows his disbelief in the existence of a Sphere.

Hence I am absolutely destitute of converts, and, for aught that I can see, the millennial Revelation has been made to me for nothing.

Prometheus up in Spaceland was bound for bringing down fire for mortals, but I—poor Flatland Prometheus—lie here in prison for bringing down nothing to my countrymen. Yet I exist in the hope that these memoirs, in some manner, I know not how, may find their way to the minds of humanity in Some Dimension, and may stir up a race of rebels who shall refuse to be confined to limited Dimensionality.

That is the hope of my brighter moments. Alas, it is not always so. Heavily weighs on me at times the burdensome reflection that I cannot honestly say I am confident as to the exact shape of the once-seen, oft-regretted Cube; and in my nightly visions the mysterious precept, "Upward, not Northward," haunts me like a soul-devouring Sphinx. It is part of the martyrdom which I endure for the cause of the Truth that there are seasons of mental weakness, when Cubes and Spheres flit away into the background of scarce-possible existences; when the Land of Three Dimensions seems almost as visionary as the Land of One or None; nay, when even this hard wall that bars me from my freedom, these very tablets on which I am writing, and all the substantial realities of Flatland itself, appear no better than the offspring of a diseased imagination, or the baseless fabric of a dream.